OMEGA POINT - INSIDE THE SPACE SHIPS

OSCAR
We enter a sacred space, a secret space within the confines of the CIRCLE..."

BARRY
I am a STRIVER

The CODE comes through

We need to link the telescopes
Implement to algorithm-receive & graphically visualize the signal
-read the barcode of the univers
-e-mail the galactic signal-

Then the code for the Program of evolution will be achieved-

Get to the Source Code of Earth Endeavor

BACKSTORY - ALIENS IN THE ROTUND

Heating sword, pulled out smoking, producing real danger

The hardest daggers are the emotional ones you don't see

SAUCERS OF THE ABSURD

THE LIVING THEATER

Alien impressario really messed up a show ruining an entire constellation of
star planets
The Order of Orion he wears an honor garter - he must bring the Show in on
Earth "The Wart" to get it done right -

They like it - think it amusing - it will get better the more you know about
your subject

He really needs the show to work. Earth needs the Show to work - there is a
show and an Anti-Show.

Market segmentation - cost per thousand -

The Anti-Show is the undermining of reality by the Marong Stewart forces,
the Brigade and Powersteeds. The bad alien Grays have taken over middle
management and have set people against each other over the centuries as
the Bildenberg Group, the Illuminati, the Cable Cabal, the media master
contrabators of wasted and unfocussed energy.

Teddy runs for Office as a way to offset the evils of the bipolar alien world - n a take on Obama's futile attempt to create leadership based on the same old system...

ADELE

We're not in Kansas anymore

Scrap of paper
SCAR v was

I am the ONE that you LOVE - as long as you give it to ME it will go around - We want to hit some serious chords with your audience - to be enlighten Ned you must first lighten up

Teddy: "We need trains-Warren says yes-We need to go beyond the mortgage system, not the MONEY system - money as leaves on the tree- we need real healthy food-there is too much that is not right in the global marketplace - we need real contact and real exchange-

MISSION StAtement

OSCAR
Don't bother me with that malarkey - get out of my Space

THE ALIEN CIRCUS MIDWAY BIG TOP - The TOP that spins - the MAGI - the magic, beauty - aloha of the visible -

OSCAR
KARAOKE - "Off Key"

OK here we go with the whole human comedy -

They like to sing we will start winging with SINGING - they will rise like their FEE NIX.

NIX THE fee

I will pick the name of the SONG and it will become the JINGLE!

OSCAR waves the WAND the sign changes

RICK'S CAFÉ GALAXY

OSCAR
Of all the gin joint saucers in the universe, the dame has to come into mine -

He waves again - the sign returns to CACTUS CAFE

March 9, 2011 - the date on the Mayan calender where we enter the "9th Wave." This vital cusp begins the "Universal Wave Movement - The Wind of Unity Consciousness," which leads to the last culmination point of the Mayan Calendar

MUSIC CUE
You can't produce a movie on coconuts -

SAUCER SONG THEME a-f-f-d

IT just has to go in MOVEMENTS like a symphonic piece -

Major thematic ELEMENTS combined together

INTRO.

Big Ship movies. Titanic. Etc. Big Top, big tent. Superdome. Sports & stadium evolution. It's a state of mind...

It's about MEDIA it's about JESUS it's about Transition it's about Everything

THE EYE=the saucer=the transition

THE SCRAP OF PAPER SCENARIOS

DISSOLVE MONTAGE: Happy cabbage, dinero, bankrolls, put it down, C-note, G-notes, filthy lucre,

STOCK FOOTAGE

"Hurdey Gurdey Man" plays on the soundtrack - accompanied by a montage of diStreSSed humanity - breadlines, hitchhikers - yoga masters - renunciates - A vacant Wall Street -

ANIMAL CRACKERS

The code it's all in the code what insurance do you have? An EBT driven subsidy economy - the lowest dollar denominator puts people out of business Big Brother steps in and takes over Mark of the Beast - all your tastes preferences and buying patterns stored on the hard drive, the distributed clloud, the orbital archive, the galactic net - the Ansarak Record

MRS KALABASH -

Figuring our the Code and the Seal of the Saucer - initialized audience members move toward the exits but are now extending the saucer into the real" probable world -

BARRY cracks the code of the saucer, dismantles the money-grab, the chlorophyl grab of the planet green-gobblers the alien spiraling - all the things in the Mattrix become unshackled, opening up to design & intention - money becomes abundant rather than scarce - suddenly there is a Trasition, a revelation, following the Tribulation and the Visitation becomes the Second Saving -

TEDDY
Get ready for some magic to happen - something truly memorable - if your memory still works after this -

Down through all eternity the crying of humanity -
Was then that the hurdy gurdy man came singing songs of Love..."

PAN UP and through the sky to;

SAUCER THEATER SHIP
Calliope music

13/20 combination RM 2220

An equation written on the back of a moldable scrap of paper.

It reads L=Ihr

Zoom IN ON A point in space which grows a TRIANGLE

"OSCAR" BRANCA DE LA VEGA an Orinion alien Ashtar Commander is seen though the viewpoint reclining on an inflight tanning bedd

He is talk, svelte, wearing tanning glasses - hence the elongated black eyes
IT'S A CHRISTMAS STORY

The SCOUT SHIP plummets down to the RIVERSIDE KAFÉ & KARAOKE bar

OSCAR
The IAM Group will play "Are You Ready'

DJ
Haven't heart it

OSCAR
Pre-digital - I wrote it - on the way in

DJ shrugs
hymykmiykuku6

EXT. KANSAS HIGHWAY.

ADELLE, lost in the field of semi's, 18-wheelers. SAUCeR goes by overhead
Markee lights flashing -

SCRAP OF PAPER falls to the ground

There are equations written on it- a sequence of code

Thje jingle ON THE RADIO - Pandora's Box - Napster -

"YOU SET YOUR OWN LEVEL OF CONSCIOUSNESS
You establish your own comfort zone and live in it

Overview - contrayor, cell magnet, corrimeter, contro, central

MAGES are MAGIS

Magic is IMAGES

The IMAGE of EARTH in the future is what you need to work on

OSCAR
We will TRANSFORM this planet -

The CIRCUS SPIRIT BODY

Login error occured. Please check user id and password, refill account or
contact the system administrator.

Take the experience o the past three months put it to music & make it rock -
half

ANIMAL CRACKERS -

RICK'S CAFÉ GALAXY

OSCAR
Out of all the gin joints in the world, the dame has to walk into mine -

STARBUCKS -
Their smiles are phoney - Phoney Baloney was the name of the Star Child

When you're ugly being nice is important

This God forsaken rock-pile

Called The Wart on all the star charts

A fester in the galactic web - and they think they're self-centric

Or charismatic when without US there is no Charisma!

TEDDY in woods with LAPTOP. Light from the LAPOP illuminating their faces.

OSCAR
We need to get your Teddy back.

Gwen
He won't come back easily.

OSCAR
You I can transform - you can learn to be a real EVOLVED woman -

OSCAR
Looking down the corridor of time - into the tunnel of LOVE - all love, all happiness, all abundance, in a big galactic deep dish SETI pie! We will serve no wine before its time. NOW is your time.

AGAIN, THE GREAT MASTER

OSCAR
It's a mosaic, the tiles of the saucer, the multi multi--D dimensional shift of the Transition

OSCAR
What do we do with this - the most important juncture in the species' history

OSCAR
So many of you have the wrong idea about religion, God - even us -

We have set up a system for global abundance - all can sign into it -

It is no good for us to do it for you, you must do it for yourselves - EVOLVE - beyond the money system, into abundance -

TEDDY
I don't see where your good intentions lie

OSCAR
Money like leaves on a tree - each leaf a metronic unit - al of nature a rich parimutuel environment - we demonstrated this with your casinos - the ships and the number games done up with lights -

OSCAR
Where does light come from? The sun? Where does the sun's light come from? Creation?

TEDDY
Besides the Ruse, there's more isn't there?

OSCAR
Only what you create.

TEDDY
Don't put it back on me

Marong Stewart is You - the other side of the coin -

OSCAR spins coin

TEDDY
You can create anything.

OSCAR
You're the one who ran. You put yourself in the bigger Loop

TEDDY
What goes around comes around -

OSCAR
We have trouble with you Earth Women - you put us through so much just for a little CONTACT!

To AUIENCE

Since you are fascinated with your sex sumbols, your -

Gwen and TEDDY and OSCAR

EXT. NIGHT. "THE GROVE" - SAUCER FIRE DANCING - IMPLANTED ON INTERIOR STAGE

OSCAR
We come to a secret place, a pace within the confines of the circle, a place where all is revealed. Join hands, please.

AUDIENCE MARKS join hands.

OSCAR
There are thorny questions about the origin of darkness and light in the universe. If darkness and light are in harmony, why are they so opposed? Are they in harmony with Life, Time - Desire?

OSCAR in the center of huge double-ring of seats.

OSCAR
In a moment we will go into the fire. Your faith will keep you from harm's way. You will believe in yourselves and the universe will believe in you.

OSCAR
Human misery can be summed up in one statement. Men and women who should naturally harmonize with and compliment each other go to battle over nothing. And there is a lot of nothing in the universe to offset the something,

OSCAR
That is why the universe does not fill up with light, and why your lives do not fill up with Love.

Int DAY
In the Hub of the Saucer Program. January Birdfoot, codename.

BARRY
You Can't use me.

I will dismantle this saucer economy. Here's the code the code is in the cards - the cards are in the Code - there is an underlying 13-base numerical system which can phase-flip back - we can VARY the RADIX and get free!

J5466784

AIDE
They will not get away with using me or my green or my green to reach their ends

I will END them first. ON WITH THE SHOW

TIME & THE TECHNOSPHERE

13-Moon Calendar

Reference

INSIDE THE SPACCESHIPS HAVE LANDED ON THE KILLING FLOOR OF THE
EXCHANGE

iMAGE
The FOTOG is the magi-MAGE

The multi-D DAEMON in the SUCER

OSCAR
Money has made you too distant White Trash

TEDDY
I got the

 Okay I have the code.

Aint no trash in my trailer NOW-

TEDDY
Get out of my house. Get off my planet.

OSCAR
Oh YOUR planet is it now? Why- because you're president of the world?

THE SEAL OF THE SAUCER
Closing down

OSCAR
You need to bring your planet home. I need to bring this SHOW home.

THE HOLOGAME

The cavernous overhead dome of the saucer lights up and erupts with

Figures, friezes of family figures - like an aerial Thansgiving gathering -
ADELLE

RODNEY
We have to work together. That's the message.

Same planet. Same saucer. What goes around comes around. Get off the square, into the circle.

BARRY
To get to the result.

OSCAR
There is no I in Fuck You.

OSCAR melts down, splits into two identities - the ABUNDANCE ALIEN and THE BEAST OF FRACTAL DRAGON

RODNEY

Groupmind. To the MAX.

The Heist is going on - they are taking our old money and replacing it with - blank LEAVES?

BILL
THAT'S ALIEN.

RODNEY
TEAM. Like the Alien guy was saying

Alton
There is no "I" in Fuck You.

BARRY
Alien is just a con man

BILL
Not entirely. He's only part THE PART THAT'S HUMAN.

ADELLE
Heart and soul. Can't win hearts and minds

WORLD WIDE WAR - DIAGRAM - ELDDERS put oon the front line on computers -

WISH ON A STAR
OSCAR
Hey gang-

TEDDY
You consorting with my wife?

OSCAR

I love my wife but Oh You Kid.

THE SHARING

ADELLE's superset tilts back, a laser light like a dentist drill burrows into her
- all the people in the concentric rings are BONDED with the bright laser
beams

OSCAR
There is only one person here - and we all Love You.

THE DANCE OF SHIPS IN SPACE

Starshine on ADELLE's face as she looks up into the vault of the saucer to
see the VISION of all 1200 saucer "dancing" in space.

Cell Magnet
CALL TO ACTION

DELUGE & FINAL JUDGEMENT

The BRAIN CLOUD forms with synapses of lightning within the AMNEOTIC
sensory conduction fluid.

People connect with the DATABASE OF THE DEAD SOUL SAUCER.

The Cell Magnet sweeps around stirring up the waters. GLOWING

FRACTAL DRAGON

The AVATAR RABBIT

Shutting down. Getting ready for the Transition.

OSCAR
The Morning of the Magicians

 http://news.yahoo.com/s/yblog_upshot/20101030/en_yblog_upshot/stewar
t-knocks-media-political-class-at-d-c-rally

I have space cadets who say they see ships all the time -

SPACE CAMP - STONER CAMP

God Bless us all Tiney Tim!

"These are your Biblical 'fallen angels'—the human ones who fell from a higher state of life
and sowed the original seeds for the conditions whic2i you now find existing in your world.

"For a long time after bringing these people to Earth, our people of many worlds visited them
often, helping and guiding them as much as they would permit. But they were a haughty and
defiant lot, and did not welcome the help we offered. Nevertheless, after the early clashes, for

a long time they managed to live well enough with one another. At that time Earth was indeed
a 'Garden of Eden,' since everything was plentiful and nature was lavish with her gifts of
food and the necessities of life.

"In the joy of the new world, these newcomers began to dwell in peace and happiness with
one another, and there was rejoicing on other planets. Then, as your Bible relates it, man ate
of the fruit of the tree of 'knowledge of good and evil,' and divisions entered where before
there had been none. Greed and possessiveness again became rampant amongst men and they
turned one against the other.
"As time went on and the population increased, out of the original tribes arose self-exalted
men who began to differentiate between the several races. Each demanded the rulership of the
whole people, professing to have come from a planet further advanced than all the others, and
by that right entitled to the ruling power. "We continued to visit these erring brothers, always
with the hope of helping them to return to a brotherly relationship. As time went on, however,
the self -appointed rulers became more and more powerful, and our efforts of less and less

avail. The divisions continued and increased, finally resulting in the establishment of what
you today call 'nations."
"The establishment of nations further separated brother from brother, and the whole of
mankind lived no longer by the Divine law. "As a result of these divisions; many different
ways of worship arose. But even then we continued to send others out in the hope of aiding
our brothers on Earth. These men were those known as 'messiahs,' and their mission was to
help their Earthly brothers to return to their original understanding. In each instance, a few
followers would gather around these wise ones, but always they were destroyed by those
whom they had come to serve. "You have wondered why Earth is the lowest planet in our
system within a Universe of which we are all inhabitants. I have now told you.
93
"The people on all worlds which have been developed by men and women who volunteered
for such service have gone steadily ahead. They have lived as the Infinite Creator intended
that His children should live. They have grown and expanded in fulfilling the will of the
Father. And each time that a group of volunteers leaves their own world to venture forth into a
new one, after the Divine Hand has prepared it for human habitation, they are actually
entering a new school of experience whereby they gain still greater understanding of a total
Universe. Thus they fit themselves for continuous advancement into higher and higher states
of expression and service.
"Labor such as you know on Earth has no part in their life, for as soon as the inhabitants of
any planet work under the will of their Creator, the elements in turn begin to serve them.
"On Earth you have just the reverse. For, through self-exaltation and the perversion of natural
law, man turns the elements against himself. Man warring against man is one of the most
obvious examples of this, as he directs destructively the energies intended by his Creator for
his welfare.
"And that is the primary difference between Earth's inhabitants and the peoples of other
planets. Earth man has repeatedly attained certain peaks, only to enter into another stage of
destruction which, through misuse of the elements, has destroyed all that he has

accomplished.

"Here and there, an individual lifts himself above the majority on your world, since it is left to
each man to speed up or slow down his own evolvement. Only when Earth men learn, by their
own mistakes, that what they look upon as their strength is really weakness when pitted
against the All-Divine Intelligence, and that their 'wisdom' but confusion against the All-
Knowledge, will they be ready to return to the fold.

"Meanwhile, we keep ourselves ever alerted to receive the call for whatever help men of
Earth may truly desire, for they are still our brothers."

"Do you never become discouraged," I asked, "in the face of such overwhelming odds?"

It was Firkon who said, "We know nothing of what you call discouragement. That is a
negative word. Long ago we learned the power of faith and hope, and of never giving up. The
goal lost yesterday can be won tomorrow. This does not mean that we believe ourselves
developed to the fullest extent. Far from it. We have eternity yet to travel. But on our worlds,
we no longer have sickness or poverty, as you know it; nor crime, as you know it. We
recognize man as the highest representation of Deity, the consummation of all lesser forms.
Should we with hurtful intent harm any form, we know that we would be forcing that form to
turn from its natural purpose and do us harm. "You can see why the Creator has left us all to
work out our own problems. When His laws are disobeyed, they witness against us. "You
speak of satan as though he were a separate en-my. But only by opposing the Divine principle
can one create the inharmonious conditions which you have credited to satan, and which you
yourselves must correct. Then you will find that satan becomes an angel of light, as your
Scripture tells you. For all distortion must be corrected by the one who distorts."

As Firkon paused, Ramu's mouth curved in the slight, grave smile so characteristic, as he
said, "The Sun rules not the Earth; nor does the Earth rule the Sun; nor do the stars rule each
other. All are ruled by the Father. Here, from nature herself, does man begin to learn." For

94

some reason, this called to mind a subject on which I had long pondered. "In regard to what
we call death and rebirth," I asked, "should we be able to carry memories of the one life over

into the next?" Ramu answered, "That is possible in varying conscious degrees. Eternal man
forgets nothing. But the memory of things learned in a former body seldom manifests as more
than an instinctive knowledge of, or gravitation toward, certain familiar things. In his
conscious mind, Earth man has little understanding of why this is so. When such aptitudes
manifest in lesser degree, you label them talents or gifts. When present to a very marked
degree, and especially when present in childhood, you call such people prodigies.
"Your planet is functioning under what you might call a low frequency. As a result, the
growth and development of form life—and especially that of man—is slow, requiring much
time between birth and maturity. When men are born on Earth, they remain in a helpless
infantile stage for a far longer period than on other planets. By the time they have reached
manhood or womanhood, whatever memory may have come over them with them at birth is
well buried under the welter of misconceptions with which, during all those early years, they
have been filled. "Independent of natural law, man's reasoning powers are very limited. The
newcomer is crammed with the traditions and conventions of past centuries, and the positive
memory of previous experience is crowded out. Such genuine memory sometimes flashes up
from what you call the subconscious into the conscious mind, through some channel suddenly
opened. This can be caused by meeting for the first time a person whom you feel you have
known, or by the sight of a place never before visited in this life, but with which you appear to
have authentic associations and memories. "All such experiences are mystifying to most Earth
people. Yet such memories are usually true memories and the explanation very simple.
"On other planets, we do not impose such blocks on the newborn child. On the contrary,
everything is done to leave him free. We realize that each human expression is slightly
different from every other, and that the individual background of experience serves as a
foundation for the fulfilling of that particular destiny. "The frequency under which a planet
functions can be established only by the inhabitants who dwell thereon. Due to the higher
frequency of our planets, those born amongst us are not subject to the slow periods of

development from infancy to maturity as on yours. With us, an average period of
development from birth through adolescence is two years as compared with your eighteen or
more.

"You on Earth use the term 'The Law of Transmigration' in a mistaken sense. What it really
means is that when an individual on your Earth has risen above the ignorance of his brothers
into a higher understanding of life, rebirth on another planet is permitted. He will come
through with a vivid memory of his experience on Earth. Predominant will be his conception
of the fundamental laws that govern all life.

Memories of his daily habits, his relationship with his family and associates, while still clear,
will be secondary. He will realize that there are no missing links between the two stages of
life, but a continuity of development uncluttered by the many names and divisions which
confused him on Earth.

"Although the climb up from infancy to maturity requires so long a period on your Earth, age
and deterioration come quickly. This is due to the old traditions and conventions which
continue to be expressed in the individual. True knowledge, no matter how long ago it was
acquired, is easily carried. But the burdens and woes of mankind repeated over and over
again, remembered through centuries, weigh insupportably on the spirit of man. "As you have

95

seen, we do not grow old in appearance or feeling. This is because we carry with us into each
fresh day the bounty of lessons well learned, discarding all that has proven sterile. As we let
the ever new and fresh express through us, we become that youthfulness.

"Just as the dream a sculptor has when he takes the clay into his hands will, when he has
finished, decide the form the clay will express, so it is with the human body. Man is the
sculptor of himself, working with materials supplied by his Creator. It is man's conception of
himself within the Universe which will mold his body and imbue his features with beauty or
with ugliness.

"In your world you picture the Deity as aged and yet eternal. This is a great contradiction, for
eternity knows no age.

"Because of the endless activity going on within the depths and on the surface of your oceans,

they survive through time. But a pond, wherein activity ceases, begins to show age by a mass
of foreign matter that slowly dims its once clear waters. What you call stagnation has
occurred.

"Bodily illness and disintegration derive from much the same process. Because you have not
learned to live by natural law, personal stagnation sets in. Occasionally, even in your world,
an individual can attain great age by your standards and still give the impression of youth.
This is due to an ability to preserve the qualities of mental activity, interest and enthusiasm
beyond the average.
I recalled a few such people I had known and nodded agreement. "You have indeed
progressed far beyond us," I said. "Is it even to the point where your progress f or-ward is
never broken?"
This caused Firkon to smile. "Far from it! But when we make mistakes they serve as lessons
for our future behavior rather than something to hide or try to justify. Moreover, when any
new territory is being explored, whether physical or of the mind, we accept some error as
inevitable. To you, what you call failure is shameful and often exposes individuals or groups
to the ridicule and censure of others. This is a primary factor in binding Earth people to old
ruts when, had they the courage, or their fellow men enough tolerance, they would try new
ways. On our worlds, no man who sincerely tries is ever considered a failure, no matter what
the results. That man has learned something. Through his very failure, he can make a great
contribution to his fellow man. Courage and enterprise have led him to try a new path which,
if proven wrong, need not again be trod by others. He alone has suffered willingly, and we,
his brothers, commend him."
As Firkon stopped speaking and glanced at Ramu, I knew that this fruitful talk was at an end.
Nothing needed to be said as we rose from the booth. We settled the bill and were again out
on the street.
This time Firkon and Ramu did not accompany me back to the hotel. "I am very grateful," I
said as we took leave of one another, the words sounding inadequate to my own ears.
I stood for a moment, watching them walk away, then turned in the opposite direction toward
my hotel.

12

AGAIN, THE GREAT MASTER

Not long after our conversation in the café, again following an impression, I found myself en
route to Los Angeles. All during the drive to that city, I was filled with a kind of joyous
anticipation that was like the remembered excitement I used to experience as a child just
before Christmas.
The mental communications from my friends of other planets were becoming more and more
definite as time went on. I knew now, for example, that this encounter would not be confined
to a restaurant on the ground, but that they would again carry me up in one of their ships.
In this happy mood, the familiar beauty of the mountains through which we rode during the
first part of the journey seemed enhanced to even greater majesty. And the valleys, surfaced
with golden yellow in the natural state, or a shining green where cultivated, filled me with
love for this Earth of ours. Surely, if mankind could learn only to look upon it with new eyes,
there could be no room left for bitterness and strife.
The time passed more quickly on this drive. I registered at the hotel, went briefly to my room,
then returned to the lobby.
Although the clock above the desk showed the time to be only a little after 5 P.M., and I
certainly was not hungry, I felt strongly impelled to go now for something to eat at the little
restaurant, then return to wait for my friends. This I did and when, close to six o'clock I was
again about to enter the hotel, Ramu stepped up to me.
I greeted him with delight and asked if I had kept him waiting.
"Not at all," he said, "I knew when to expect you!"
The Pontiac was parked by the curb around the corner. As we got in, I asked about Firkon.
"He is unable to come with us this time," Ramu said, "and asked me to tell you that he is
sorry to miss seeing you.
The mood of sustained happiness and anticipation remained with me all during the long drive
out of Los Angeles and beyond. Occasionally, we exchanged a few words but for the most
part there was little conversation.
Eventually we turned off the main highway and bumped along over a narrow road for perhaps
half an hour. Searching the darkness for a first glimpse of the Scout, at last I saw a faint glow

in the distance. As the outline became clearer, I knew from its size that it must be the
Saturnian Scout, or a similar ship.
97
It was the same, and Zuhl was there to greet us. The journey to the hovering mother ship was
quickly over. "Is this … ?" I began, and Zuhl smiled and nodded, "The Saturnian ship you
were on before? —Yes." The landing procedure was accomplished exactly as on the previous
visit. As Zulu led me in the direction of the large lounge, he paused a moment and said, "It
was the master himself who asked that we bring you tonight. This visit is entirely that he may
talk to you. If it was possible for my joy to mount higher, it did so on hearing this.
On entering, I was struck anew with the beauty of this room, and the harmony that filled it.
All whom I had met before were present, and no strangers except for two beautiful women
who resembled one another closely enough to be twins. I guessed, before introductions were
made, that these were Satumian women. On the right sleeves of their blouses, near the
shoulder, were the same insignia I had seen on the shirts of the Saturnian men on the last visit.
After my friends had welcomed me, I exchanged greetings with the two lovely strangers.
There were differences both in their persons and garments from those of the other women.
Since they remained standing close to me, I had an opportunity to check these in detail. Both
women had very dark brown hair and eyes, and thick curling lashes. The complexions were of
an almost startling whiteness with a rose cast in the cheeks; the lips were full and red. Both
appeared to have a greater vivacity of manner than the other women. I believe, however, that
this had nothing to do with the fact that they were Saturnians, but was rather a characteristic
of their own personalities.
They wore light-blue blouses with long, full sleeves drawn in tightly at the wrists. These
blouses were more like short jackets and were finished at the neck with a narrow rolled collar.
The skirts were of the same color and material. The latter appeared very light in texture and of
a quite different weave from any I had seen. The full skirts had wide waistbands and were
ankle length, like those of the other women. They wore fawn-colored sandals on their small
feet.

I did not see the master and presumed that the reason all remained standing was in expectation
of his entrance.
"There is quite a bit of activity on the part of your air force tonight," Ramu told me, "and the
ship is now rising. We shall probably remain hovering at about ninety thousand feet from
your Earth."
Needless to say, I did not feel, nor had I felt, any movement whatsoever.
At this point the master entered and all turned toward him.
As his eyes met mine, he smiled and walked on to where a table was surrounded by low chairs
with arms, 2overed with attractively upholstered material of an appearance something like
dull silk.
Ramu led me over and the master indicated that I take the place on his right. One of the
Saturnian ladies sat on my other side and while the people were settling into their seats, I
seized the opportunity to ask if she could explain the meaning of the insignia. She obligingly
twisted around so that I could examine the one on her right shoulder and said, "It denotes that
Saturn is the Tribunal of this system." Although I did not know exactly what she meant by
"tribunal," she did not explain further. The design consisted of a sphere encircled by a ring
98
(much as the ringed planet appears through our telescopes), and inside the sphere was a
balanced pair of scales.
Thanking her, I settled back into my chair and found it difficult to believe that anything could
be so comfortable. Not even our air cushions yield to and yet support the body as did that
chair. The master began to speak. "My son, if some of what you will hear tonight seems
repetitious, it is because the things of which I shall speak are important to your understanding,
and perhaps a fuller explanation will help you to retain them."
I was glad to hear him say this, since, even with the telepathic help which had been promised
me, I still worried for fear I might not remember it all.
"A great fallacy which has grown on the people of Earth," the master said, "is the custom of
dividing into many parts that which should never be divided. You have multiple divisions in
forms and teachings, many firm likes and dislikes, all of which serve only to add to the state
of confusion on your planet.
"We of other worlds have no such divisions but realize the relationship and the

interdependence of all things. I know that you have felt deeply the power and radiance of our
conception of Deity there on the wall before you. By keeping always this image visual before
our eyes, and remembered in our hearts, we never forget that within Him all forms have their
being.

"He is the giver of what you call life' unto men. He is also the giver of life through us to our
creations in which He is the instructor of what is to be created. He it is who knows how the
minerals and the elements are to be combined—not only to serve us, but the Universe as well,
ever better as they are brought up through the experiences of one form, to be fitted for a
higher form. We on Venus, and on other planets in varying degrees of evolvement, recognize
the minerals and elements as the essence of ever-active Divine expression, with a steady
newness. And therefore monotony, as you know it on Earth, can never be.

"So, as the creation of a Divine Creator of the total Universe is respected by us, so also is the
creation of man who guides the elements in different channels of service likewise respected
and honored. In turn, the elements become desirous to serve better each day that they, too,
may rise to a higher standard of service . . . a service which shall never cease, for it is eternal.

"As an example, that you may understand this more clearly, the bit of iron which you find
among the minerals of your Earth serves you in one particular channel. Yet by impregnating
this iron with a force which you call 'electricity' the iron changes from a previous service to
another type of service called 'magnetic.' Therefore it has been endowed with a power of
attraction which it did not have before. This is what we mean by elements or minerals
evolving for a better service. For first it was merely the mineral iron; then it reached a higher
state of service where it was able to attract, which in the original state it could not do. And so,
on and on, this iron can evolve toward higher and higher service rendered unto its Creator.

"So you see what is meant when I speak of the minerals and the other elements serving man.
By doing this, they themselves are endowed with certain powers of comprehension through
serving the All-inclusive Intelligence. This law, I believe, is known to you on Earth as the
Law of Transmutation, or the Law of Evolution.

99

"A human body like yours and mine is composed of elements as well as minerals. And you
can prove that these elements and minerals which compose your body do obey the
impressions placed upon them. For if the impressions are of a joyous nature, the being called
'man' is joyful. But if of an angry state, then the body expresses that, proving that the
minerals and the elements within it are constantly serving the Intelligence. Without it they
cannot rise to a higher state of expression.
"You men of Earth continually invite disaster by creating combinations which are opposing
each other rather than working together. You have made of yourselves something other than
your Divine origin. You have added many false concepts to your being instead of remaining
natural; like a beautiful woman who is exalted in beauty, yet adds many trinkets that finally
exalt themselves above her beauty. "You have done the same by adding that which had no
true life or intelligence. Let me point out to you something inherent in the being of man by
which we live on the planet Venus, while you do not, though these principles apply to yours
as well as other worlds.
"You claim that you are a being made up of five senses, and list others to be added—the sixth,
seventh, and so on. You seek to develop these arbitrarily conceived senses instead of
understanding and developing those which do exist. In professing that there are powers of
clairvoyance, clairaudience, mental telepathy, or extra-sensory perceptions, you thereby
divide one total phase of expression into at least four separate classifications. And, as a result,
your true identities

"A human body like yours and mine is composed of elements as well as minerals. And you
can prove that these elements and minerals which compose your body do obey the
impressions placed upon them. For if the impressions are of a joyous nature, the being called
'man' is joyful. But if of an angry state, then the body expresses that, proving that the
minerals and the elements within it are constantly serving the Intelligence. Without it they
cannot rise to a higher state of expression.
"You men of Earth continually invite disaster by creating combinations which are opposing

each other rather than working together. You have made of yourselves something other than
your Divine origin. You have added many false concepts to your being instead of remaining
natural; like a beautiful woman who is exalted in beauty, yet adds many trinkets that finally
exalt themselves above her beauty. "You have done the same by adding that which had no
true life or intelligence. Let me point out to you something inherent in the being of man by
which we live on the planet Venus, while you do not, though these principles apply to yours
as well as other worlds.
"You claim that you are a being made up of five senses, and list others to be added—the sixth,
seventh, and so on. You seek to develop these arbitrarily conceived senses instead of
understanding and developing those which do exist. In professing that there are powers of
clairvoyance, clairaudience, mental telepathy, or extra-sensory perceptions, you thereby
divide one total phase of expression into at least four separate classifications. And, as a result,
your true identities

we know the history of your world well. The conception of 'We are our brother's
keeper' applies to all mankind everywhere. It is in this role that we come to you and say, 'Let
the Supreme Being of the Universe be the guiding word for your world that your troubles may
vanish as darkness before light.' "What would man be without the breath of life? And who
giveth unto him? Is it not to be found everywhere for the benefit of all? Then let Earthly man
know that his God is not in some far distant place, but ever near

OLD KARAOKE SCRIPT

 March 9, 2011 - the date on the Mayan calender where we enter the "9th Wave." This vital cusp begins the "Universal Wave Movement - The Wind of Unity Consciousness," which leads to the last culmination point of the Mayan Calendar

SAUCER SONG THEME a-f-f-d

IT just has to go in MOVEMENTS like a symphonic piece -

Major thematic ELEMENTS combined together

INTRO.

Big Ship movies. Titanic. Etc. Big Top, big tent. Superdome. Sports &
stadium evolution. It's a state of mind...

We came to earth to save it from itself - Disneyland Delight - Cosmic Circus -
level of realization. Place in the universe. Universe as holographic, will
support you (and me) We are all in the same "saucer" - the round table of
the global earth trying to steer in a collective direction.

It's about MEDIA it's about JESUS it's about Transition it's about Everything

THE EYE=the saucer=the transition

DISSOLVE MONTAGE: Happy cabbage, dinero, bankrolls, put it down, C-
note, G-notes,

"Hurdey Gurdey Man" plays on the soundtrack - accompanied by a montage
of diStreSSed humanity - breadlines, hitchhikers - yoga masters -
renunciates - A vacant Wall Street -

TEDDY
Get ready for some magic to happen - something truly memorable - if your
memory still works after this -

Down through all eternity the crying of humanity -
Was then that the hurdy gurdy man came singing songs of Love..."

PAN UP and through the sky to;

SAUCER THEATER SHIP
Calliope music

PRESS CONFERENCE, Washington

EST and ACTUAL

Holly Moley - spare change you can believe in - give me a break -m

MCBAIN
This is the beginning of the rapture?The Incarnation of God?

Brenda of American Airlines
Murshida Va

Air Card - early technology -

MT SHASTA
NeW Ager Agent New Agent Sex & sin-Phony
I'm right there with you

PAN RIGHT out to the stars – there a triangle forms and explodes
with a glowing tetrahedral cluster of 1,280 SAUCERS coming through the
void, leaving a "scenic boom" -

MAUI TELESCOPE-ASTROPHYSICISt
...beautiful colors

INT. SAUCER

OSCAR
Viewscreen, display on the wall
Who's the evolution star of them all

Through the CIRCULAR view port

OSCAR-ASHTAR DeVEGA ("of Vega") is a Vegas-style alien, complex,
charismatic, "crazy" like a Groucho Marx figure, trying to bring the Show
home for the Angels - win one for the Gipper. He had a Bad Show on one of
the other systems, and has to retrieve his reputation

OSCAR
Womb=Memory - now, where was I?

Show us your Lark Pack – send in the dove of Peace.
Have a good day – and that's an order.
Green Peace RV park - now THAT's where I want to stay

New technology appears every day. Add up to it.

They're behind you.

GREEN PEACE RV PARK. DAY

OSCAR drives up an a beatup Pinto

There is a BAR next door with sign:

KARAOKE close on signup: "1-Alien Band"

OSCAR with a side pack, on stage - crazy music - he sings VO

Crowd: cheers hoops

Stage Musician

What was THAT we just played?

First of many "around the world" sequences - the SOUND is sent to the WIRES to the SATELLITE down to Pandora to ADELLE's couch-side Walkman - she hears the JINGLE

ADELLE
Huh? Hello?

"MNY CHOZN FW CALD"
This is a hot pop hi-hop alien tune

ADDELLE gets up from the couch the B&W TV is on suddenly bursts into color: the ALIEN SPOT

TNT: Sequence:

WALLET, CROWN for Queen for the Day (GWEN),

Tetrahedral DIAMOND formations, the Event Horizon on stage within the saucer - MERKABA displays - the ascending light patterns on the stage - alien evolution machinery - set to run with the audience.

BANK kaka loans money withheld, no money available, without a supple loan market, value must surely fall

Roll of the DICE

CLOVER

OSCAR (VO)
Parimutuel environment - we need to teach them - how to share energy and time as well as what they call MONEY

BILLS as in dollar bills and Bills Gate

STAR

The Pleaides Subaru SEVEN sisters cluster

ROLL on the highway, around the planet, into the roller derby, the spiral vortex in the SAUCER

HORSESHOE, locomotive, to ponder a motive, the engine of the saucer is computational, rotational -

CHIPS are value and the roulette of the saucer let's everyone ante up, then take their chips and go home. The aliens chop off your hands at the wrists as you go for your chips,

APPLE computer becomes like the ESTATE II example in movie a big MBAG
Moneybag

I have no idea - a black phone

Carnegie MELON university

You're sad
I'm glad
You all want clover

OSCAR
Tripping on trauma, life becomes melodrama -
The hardest sin to be is original

WHAT PRICE LOVE?
The good times are over
The honey and clover are...GONE
You never told me the fee when you gave it to me....

The HORSESHOE of GOOD LUCK need to be rightside Up

She has nice MELONS AD DELLE DOES

CHERRY RING BERRY - GRAB AT THE FRUIT LOOP

BUSBY BERKELEY MUSIC SHOWSTOPPER

12 SCREEN AD CAMPAIGN

Superstar Porn Game - she decides to go down on the mike like a sex worker
would on a cock - ADELLE HUIT French Songstress - HARDY

ELDER
This one - Wright - the one who escaped-

OSCAR
Couldn't take the input -

ELDER
Got to get him back - the numerology is very precise

OSCAR
I know -

ELDER

Without his tile in the mosaic the Show might spin out the other way - into
total failure

OSCAR
This is the last brick in the galactic house -

THE MONEY GAME SHOWSTOPPER
Stop the show - yea - sure

MAKE Sure it HAS HEART

We are all the

OSCAR
Money separates and limits - unless there is enough for everyone and for
everything...

TEDDY
Then give us back the MONEY - show me the SAUCER DOLLARS NOW

AIDE carries a portable tweaker, sets it up.

AIDE 1
Can't carry the bandwidth -- this is coming in across
the spectrum in 29 flavors, fourteen colors and thousands of frequencies -

ADELE WHEAT, in a rusty pickup truck, wearing hippie-granny dress clothing,
picks up a piece of paper floating down from the GALACTIC THEATER saucer
that goes by overhead.

It says
11:17
12:13
1280 X 10000
Hydroglyphics, equations, grocery items
Oscar Branca de La Vega

ADELLE
Water words?

TRAVEL SHOT - Department Store Windows, long line of disenfranchised

CLOSE, MONITORS -- the 17 SPOTS of the aliens are run through, "buy"
specs speed by underneath defining the saucer "buy" of media adjacencies
throughout the TV/CABLE NETWORK

TICKETS GO ON SALE FOR SAUCER SHOW - Ticketmaster

SAUCER LOTTERY - "SMART" interactive TV of the future.

ADELLE, FARO, BILL, TEDDY, GWEN, BARRY, CARL, HANNAH all have their first taste of the Saucer Spot promotion."

SAUCER LOTTERY

"Line up for the saucer lottery...take your number at the door...as you wait to get in...can you hang on to it anymore?"

SIGN: Peace!

EXT. NIGHT. GRID OF EARTH - POPULATION DENSITY CENTERS.SAUCERS move along lines of roads, highways, moving toward areas of high demographic concentration(song)Line up at the immigration...see the aliens all in line...see them go in to the saucer station...don't they all look so divine....SPINNING HEADLINES:

SAUCERS A THOUSAND SHARE
1280 SAUCER VENUES – COUNT EM

ALIEN
Louie says, where's the money? In the Marong Stewart coffers -

OVERHEAD slow montage
Crop Circles - currency symbols, appear on the fields - field of dreams

Oscar
If we don't speak enough of the same language we can't understand each other - you are like the younger generation - how are we going to communicate without communication?

Hoot mon, raster man vibration - let's get one love going on this world - got to jump start the oil cart - and get into Longevity -

Zappa-man - what's the ugliest part of your body? We are the other people you're the other people too - trying to get to you -

Marong Stewart - the alien shape shifters, the economic manipulators, the veil over the real Program - Oscar Ms addresses ...
...the BOARD

OSCAR
I hate the corporation - the corporation is dead

TEDDY
Long live the corporation

First get the right target market - give them what you want - find something in common - give them what you want & make it look like what THEY want

RODNEY and ALTON

VR gear

DAK
It's all about FAITH - your whole LIFE is faith - every day is an act of faith -

They're traveling like storm patterns, or BY the storm patterns.

OSCAR
There are no straight lines in outer space

WELCOME TO EARTH: NO WAIT FOR WEIGHT.

OSCAr
The First rule of encounter - is to LEAVE

INT CAR DAYTEDDY WRIGHT driving to work. Cellphone beeps - he answers hands free

TEDDY
Got to get OUT of here. This space is too SMALL for me.

Through the windshield he Sees the figures standing by the side of the road.

Sign: ANYWHERE BUT HERE.

WRIGHT
Yea? We'll see. We will see.

INTRODUCTION: The indistinct saucer central control arena.
The "view circle" above the main saucer stage-arena below.AIDEThis is the remote viewing to monitor what happens on the stage.OSCAROf life?

FAST DISSOLVE26 radio dish telescopes turn and cock their ears, like dogs, like Nipper...OSCAR

"His Master's Voice" - we're number One with a Bullet, climbing the charts, getting into their HEARTS and MINDS, doing the Parts - I LOVE it -
The closer you get the further you are away...

Angelo Mecino (BARRY)

There isn't just one thing there are many things - there's just one thing - your kids

Circular radio satellite dish broadcasting the JINGLE around the world -

OSCAR
We are NOW a household word! Bring us into the household

MINI MOVIE – THE BIRTHING OF HUMANITY – (Underlying theme)

MATCH CUT:

Circular PEORIA SAUCER crossing "Nevada" on the glowing map-scope.

INT. GWEN/ TEDDY'S CONDO - NIGHTGWEN before the screen of the bed TV
-- she is tossing and dreaming --

SPIRAL ZOOM in on FACE

Eyes exhibit REM of GWEN. TEDDY sleeps next to her, his eyes moving under
the eyelids.

A pyramid "super city" in the middle of North America, which has grown up
to be the largest city in the WORLD in 2011.The clouds in background move
past in fast motion, foreboding CHANGE.

GWEN and TEDDY are silent. DISSOLVE:

INT. AIRLINER -- "NIGHT" (MORE OF THE "DREAM"?)
Dozing or bored passengers, watching a movie, drinking.
GWEN with bassinet & infant – a white rabbit stuffed animal in the bassinet

 ENORMOUS light passes along the rows of passengers, like the exposure rod
of a photocopier --

The BABY disappears with the light as it crosses the space. The White Rabbit
stuffed animal holds a GLOW for a second and remains in the bassinet.

PAN UP through the airline fuselage TO the sky

Large stadium-saucer overhead, passing by

A group of dignitaries, riding in first class, have their hair pulled up straight
magnetically, their eyes glazing and dilated -- on the first-class SCREEN:

OSCAR's face appears, mouthing the words of the ALIEN JINGLE, as though
an MTV video - "Prince"-like.

OSCAR
"Are U Ready 2 Evolve, then Come On..."Words crawl by on the bottom of
the screen, Karaoke-style

AND
Around the saucer markee -

MINI-MOVIE 4 THE HEIST

ALIENS hit the KAKA bank, rounding the corner -

STRETCHED FACE -

"Cut the Cake"

ALIEN "HIERO-GRAPHICS" CRAWL (WITH TRANS.)

GWEN

TNT: DAY

GWEN
I lost the baby - did I HAVE the baby?

TEDDY
There goes our chance for any more Wrights – we were going to do the trial
adoption

OSCAR"My Cognitive Assist Coin"
OSCAR flips a coin which becomes a SPHERE in the air -

INT. DAY.

TV links, looking "through" the display TV's to see the FACES of the
AUDIENCE members of the Saucer Show to come -SAUCER LOTTERY -
"SMART" interactive TV of the future.ADELLE, FARO, BILL, TEDDY, GWEN,
BARRY, CARL WASHINGTON, MARTHA, HANNAH all have their first taste of
the Saucer Spot promotion.

ADELLE crosses her yard to the barrier of NEWROUTE 66. She climbs over
the barrier, stands there hitching. Two large SEMI's roar by. A sprinkle of
starshine, all around.OVERHEAD, a huge stadium-saucer moves by at low
altitude.On the end a license plate should be viewable: GAL-LA-2068
ADELLE (CONT'D)What did you say?"I don't think you're in Kansas
anymore?"

Jingle of laughter a laugh track in her head

INT. DAY. OFFICES OF SHIP, INC.

FARO CONSTANTIOPLE moves through his office in NEW YORK NEW WORLD
TRADE CENTER tower, on the phone.

FARO
Pinhead President. Let's the economy go on its knees to pray to his higher
POWER - information is power.

FARO

Information is bullshit. Money talks, bullshit walks.

OSCAR
They are still in the throes of a metronic value system separate from their
true selves – we need to show them how to truly evolve, they must rise
ABOVE their money system –

Through the window VIEW of the HUDSON. A passenger jet descends and
lands on the waters of the river. People begin crawling out onto the wings.

FARO
Real estate is down - the rich are buying. We are buying.

TV, computer monitors abound.FARO (CONT'D)Get me a ticket to this Show.
I want to GO.THE NYLA TIMES NEWSROOM - ALL NIGHT NEWS VIDEO
STUDIORODNEY and ALTONVideo Jockeys of the future, wear "miner"-like
hats, with video cams pointing out the front, the side panels are earphone
drop-downs.

INT. NIGHT. THE ANNN STUDIOS IN PEORIA

MEGALOPOLIS.CLOSE on TEDDY.

TEDDY
If what the saucers present is alien theater-- then we should send a
reviewer.
COPY EDITOR
But who do we send?
TEDDY$500 a ticket and no hypress comps.I don't know. What about
Willard.CEIs it a play or what?
COPY EDITOR
They call it "The Show."
TV SCREEN DISSOLVE to another TV screen, in the department store
windows near NARONG STEWART CORPORATION HEADQUARTERS.

All the spots flash by rapidly on each of the multiple TV screens in the
department store windows.

DAK WILLARD, the theater reviewer, in his mid-5O's, walks into the City
Room.TEDDYSpeak of the devil.WILLARDNo, just his assistant.TEDDYWillard,
what do you think of the saucerstory - is it a theater piece?WILLARDThey call
it The Show, right?COPY BOY(excited)Yea, the ad department got a double-
page adby satellite.WILLARDPerhaps I should just "Show up."TEDDY picks up
a large copy of the ad layout, shows it. Big block letters -- THE SHOW --
$500.TEDDYThe bottom half inch was fine print, reversed. You couldn't read
it without a magnifying glass. Almost couldn't even WITH one.

WILLARD

Who knows what to expect? Movies, dance, multi-media? Some space concoction meant to enrapture the proles. The sheeple.

If you really believe in something it is part of your life - you cannot be told it is wrong.

So maybe they are praying to the same God - in a different way - everyone WANTS the same things, praying, chanting

WE WANT TO BE UNIVERSAL & WE'RE STILL STUCK IN THIS MONEY-TRAP111

The money system special - get free for a FOTOG

It's all about the numbers - you make the payment but you still owe -

FULL SCREENA long row of placement avails comes onto the extended screen -- there are 7,992 listings, multi-columns, running down the side of the screen.Close, FACES, glassy-eyed, tired, bleary, look at the ALIEN COMMERCIAL SPOT.TRAFFIC (O.S.)That's 17 days, all media.TEDDY runs down the line of workers at their consoles.TEDDY

 AGENCY: SAUCERMAGEAVAILS: ALL
DURATION: 17 DAYSCOMMISSION: STANDARD 15%
AE: OSCAR
Fast crawl at screen bottom, O.S.NUMERICAL SEQUENCE 00000000001 -- 1100010010 * --MUST BEFOLLOWED WITHOUT VARIANCE. THIS IS A TIMED, ACCELERATED CAMPAIGN.FOR FULL SATURATION, ANY VARIANCE FROM THIS NUMERICAL SEQUENCEWILL BE SUBJECT TO IMMEDIATE MAKE-GOODS OR THERE WILL BE NO PAYMENT.THESE WILL BE MONITORED BY SAUCERMAGE.

IMAGISTIC SEQUENCE

DETAIL "through the ground" -- fiber optic, speeding through the strands, the images to the (circles) eye ---a flight through electronic media space --- the entry into the planet MEDIA GRID NETWORK BACK TO: the eye.

YOU WILL TAKE PART IN THE SHOW AND BE A PART OF YOUR PLANET'S EVOLUTION
PEOPLE running down the sidewalks of Peoria.

VISUAL: A field of wheat.

VOAs you sow, so do you reap..Worker moves through the field with a scythe.The wheat falls. The worker stands, wipes his brow, turns to the camera. His face is a skull.ZOOM IN

The skull fills the screen -- the skull is now held in a hand, the worker has become a Shakespearian actor, standing in the field, contemplating mortality.ACTORAlas, poor Yorick, I knew him well...but he worked himself to death.

DISSOLVE The skull becomes an ESTATE II computer, gleaming, a Star highlight on its organic plastic shell.

INT. TV STUDIO - DAY.

TEDDY watches the MS interview. OSCAR
Life and death. And the origin of TIME.

Do you know anything abut derivatives, about astral projection, about mortgages on a flying saucer-ship the size of a mountain - ?

We will graduate you to the Next Stage of Evolution, to the Next Level, when you are READY - we will serve no wine before its time. THE MIDWAY AROUND THE SAUCER.ALIENs - little green men mill about. "Whistle While You Work" dwarf music - these are little men - dance along next to the crowd waiting in line to go in.ALIEN HIERARCHY ditty"We are the alien hierarchyHere to take you HigherJust like archery, an arrow through the heart,We will make you feel again, what it's likeTo be together, and how painful to be apart...Come join with the Ashtar CommandWe want to save the universe from yourselves...We embrace you and the power of the Twelves"

IT IS THE WORD

TWO GREEN ALIENS in GREEN JACKETS. We want to create a campaign, an image development campaign, using kid's lollipops, charms, amulets, guitar picks, cereal packaging and bumper stickers, plus movies and personality placement, to improve the image of aliens from outer space in the minds of the population.
Cut to the chase, we sayBILLThat's a tall order, but sure - we'd love the account. Who wouldn't?OSCARMaybe you if it don't work out we have a way of getting revenge for campaigns that don't WORKBILLD-don't INTIMIDATE ME We want the account and the theme because we - or I - want to rise ABOVE media -ALIENHell no, we're even giving you COMPS to The Show.BILLWow at $500 a head that's very nice of youALIENIt's nothing - you'll come to see. We had to put a value on it. We give it all to charity. Alien charities.INT. DAY. THE LUNCH COUNTER. KANSAS.ADELLE slings hash for the Regulars.ADELLEThis is the counter culture here.TV TALKING HEADAround the saucers we see the now-familiar 3-ball landing gears on the scout ships.RANDY ROPEThree balls! Hahahahaha!ADELLEOnly time there's flying saucers around here is when I throw plates at the customers.OVERHEAD, a huge stadium-saucer moves by at low altitude.On the end a license plate should be viewable: GAL-LA-2068FARO in his offices in business office tower.VIEW of the HUDSON.TV, computer monitors

abound.FAROGet me a ticket to this Show. I want to GO."A girl in a truck in Kansas going toward the saucers – human interest – her name is Adelle – ndance on it she picks up a scap of paper with the formula for planetary abundance I it - get a story on it

MINI MOVIE 5 – The musical SHOW by the ALIENS

"We're Only Here for the Money"

OVERHEAD, a huge stadium-saucer moves by at low altitude.On the end a license plate should be viewable: GAL-LA-2068.] The CROSSROADS. There are four crop-circles in each of the field quadrants defined by the Cross Video Jockeys of the future, wear "miner"-like hats, with video cams pointing out the front, the side panels are earphone drop-downs.RODNEYLet's COVER it. Let's bust a move in the direction.ALTONYea - maybe we can become famous documentarians.

Banner:
YOU MUST RISE ABOVE YOUR MONEY SYSTEM =

OSCAR
NO MONEY NO HONEY

MARKEE
TO TRULY EVOLVE YOU MUST MOVE BEYOND YOUR MONEY SYSTEM

OSCAR
We have a Show to do.

Lope de Vega - set up your characters - oppose them irreconcilably - defy expectations and go for a resolution - is that what you mean? There are special locations - in Colorado, in

EDITORHow about if we send a reviewer.RODNEYWho is there? There's no real theater left, just sense plays, Music Videos, global hookups and 3-day survival media events.
DAK WILLARD, the old time "print" reviewer, enters the compound.DAKWhat do you get if you combine Pirandello with Lamaze?ALTONNo. What.DAKSix characters in search of an early childbirth.RODNEYHuh?CITY

EDITORSomeone needs to review the alien show for the masses.ALTONSomeone needs to review the reviewer. DAKHow about two dime-change beggars?ALTONI'm ready.DAKPair 'a dime shifters. $500 a ticket and no press comps.I don't know. Is it a play or what? EDITORThey call it "The Show." TEDDY picks up a large copy of the ad layout, shows it. Big block letters -- THE SHOW -- $500.TEDDY "ARE YOU READY?" BARRY (MUMBLING) The SAUCER appears on the screen, dwarfing the earth satellite station.It is HUGE. A "stadium saucer" with flattened sides, canted like the Coliseum. FULL SCREENA balletic display of the contours, design and configuration of he saucer in computer wire frame and full 3D modeling and color. e are treated to a guided tour of the design of the saucer, showing the interior, corridors (flashing lights), display screens, conveyor ramps, entrance, red seats, blue carpet, access c way, parking lots, surrounding midway village, exterior landscaping (moat, formal gardens, parks, fields) plus detail of he stage/lighting area, the cell magnet, the superseats, the eating wedges, the configurations of the central mechanism, the passenger/sleeping area atop the saucer interior, the pilot-like tiers with couches and instrumentation, the power supplies of :the saucer, the perimeter accelerator, the markee display, the chlorophyll and other food based storage area, the tanks which hold the sensory conducting fluid, the moveable walls and ceilings, :he laser-light projection points, etc.

DETAIL

The CELL MAGNET form flashes as the saucer interior divides into in exploded view and reassembles in computer "real time.".

RODNEYYou want to go to this?ALTONMaybe they'll assign usto cover it.RODNEYAt $500 a throw I mightpass it up unless they do.ALTONDidn't you always want to evolve -- to something different?RODNEYI just want to work and get paid.ALTONYea, that's great. For you.I don't know what it is, but I want to go -- I'll do anything.
RODNEYLook at that guy - he looksdead.ALTONYea, he'd like us all to be in heaven.RODNEYYea, as long as he gets his Rolls Royces and his whores.SKULL dissolves and becomes a small, beige-white computer with an illuminated screen of menu icons.The computer continues to spin for examination as the hand fades.
VO
The Estate II computer... one will be helping you do your work soon...

TEDDY
GET OUT OF MY HOUSE! GET OUT!

TEDDY picks up cans and boxes around the kitchen, hurling them at OSCAR.

OSCAR ducks.
OSCAR
WHAT DIDN'T YOU LIKE ABOUT THE SHOW?

TEDDY hurls the coffee can.How?OSCAR spreads his armsTEDDYYou'd better go back to Vega and get some writing lessons. Skulls sinking into mud,

screaming dancers, strobe lights. From Act One to Two Hundred.OSCARNot everyone saw what you saw. The Show -- it plays on your mind. It brings to you and you bring to it. The Show is an Exchange.TEDDYWhat about GWEN?OSCARShe was waiting on the road for he demon loverShe was a maiden oh so bold, but she had never know a suitor
TEDDY
What do you offer us for evolution?
OSCAR
The Dali Llama is was in the Ashtar Command
Now he's down on earth, leading the band.

MINI MOVIE 5 TALK SHOW: STATUS THING

OSCAR
(est-like phraseology)
What you think of me is none of my business

I am holding space for that kind of eventuality – although I think your fate will be much better –

Household: word. The word. Say the Word – Love.

We'll be in your house HOLD – what will be in your HOLD time?

DAK WILLARD
13 weeks with a PILOT - the allien "master magician" - in the SHOW-
It's a "Saucer Season"...

TWO MONITORS

INTWhat of your product - the Estate computer?

DISSOLVE TO: SWEEPING MOTION PANView over The Loop toward the MS tower, a black pyramid of steeland glass occupying ten city blocks.INT. CHICAGO/ THE MARONG STEWART BOARDROOM -- DAYO.S. THE ESTATE II SPOT continues.VOYou can turn your work time into free time.Into Play time.CLOSE on the skull, turned in the hand for examination. IT BECOMES an Estate II computer, with a fist-sized display screen, then back to the face of the actor, now facing us.ACTORThe Estate II micro computer is yourmissing link between now and the future...It weighs 3.2 pounds, and can processinformation faster than your own brain...It is a smart system, and may even think up some solutions to problems you haven't even thought of yet...The actor's face dissolves back to the skull, held in the hand, becomes the computer again.

INT. TV CONTROL - DAY

A symbiotic relationshiopo is iomplied -

TEDDY watches the MARONG STEWART interview, puzzled. "SPINNING HEADLINES" OF OLD MOVIES'TICKETS GO ON SALE FOR SAUCER SHOW'INT. NEWS OFFICE -- CITY ROOM OF CABLE NEWS NETWORK.REPORTERS stand around looking at the monitors.SPOT ON TV MONITOR.VO/Character Crawl:THE SAUCER IS YOURSELF!THE SHOW: $500 PER EARTH PERSONCOME TO WHERE THERE IS NO SEPARATION BETWEEN THE DREAMER AND THE DREAMED!MONTAGE CUTS: PENTAGON, OTHER LOCATIONSSPOTWE CHALLANGE YOU!as groups of faces watching, glued.ARE YOU READY FOR THE NEXT STEP INEVOLUTION?
SWIRL OF COLORS. HEADLINE CRAWL UNDER THE SCREEN THROUGH THE NEXT FEW SCENES, EVOKING AN "ON SCREEN" TICKERTAPE NEWS SERVICE.EXT. DAY.A crowd watches the SPOTS from a city street.BACKGROUND: A department store, with a sign saying: LOST LEASE, LAST DAYS SALE: 200% OFF EVERYTHING! EVERYTHING MUST GO!MAKE NORTH EAST WEST SOUTH WORK FOR YOU// WE CAN WORK TOGETHER TOWORK IT OUT AND MAKE IT WORK// WORK IT OUT, EARTH PEOPLE// DOESIT WORK?// WORK FOR MONEY AND MAKE MONEY WORK!// COME TO THESAUCER// WE LIVE IN AN AGE OF TRANSPORTATION/I WE WORK TO GETFROM HERE TO THERE// TRANSPORTATION IS CIVILIZATION// COME TOTHE SHOW/ BE TRANSPORTED TO NEW WORLD-YOU WILL EVOLVE

TEDDY
I'm just trying to make a buck - and the buck keeps slipping away -
Into the future...

INTERIOR. BILL EVANS AGENCY -

BILL is portly 40's ish Irish English dude with a beard and a smart attitude

BILL
This is like the Second Coming with Saucers -

ALTON
Like McBain's Rapture

Jesus was the greatest ad campaign of all time

DAY EXT. THE BIG BUY SHOPPING MALL - LATERBART (12) and BARRYBARTWhat's the Show?BARRYThat's the question everyone's asking. Daddy wishes he knew.WIDER ANGLE SHOWING:TEDDY and GWEN stand near the kiosk. BARRY and SHIELA come forward.TEDDYWhat do you say. You going to this Show?

BARRYYou bet. I'll evolve and getbetter commissions.Yea, sure.SH I ELA

BARRYHow about you, Gwen?GWENI don't know.SHIELA(sarcastically)Yea, you've got to do it. If we can,anyone can do it.TEDDYHow difficult it is to get --women to take things seriously. $5000 IS A SMALL PRICE. 2 BE PART OF THE NEXT STEP. THE NEXT EVOLUTION...MULTI-SCREEN:Change to: EACH OF THE MAIN 12 CHARACTERS' FACES AS THE SPOTS (5) PLAY, introducing their faces to the audience, in a "face grid" like Hollywood Squares.FARO, FOSS, ADELLE, BARRY, SHIELA, GWEN, TEDDY, RODNEY, ALTON, SAX, EGO, DAK, watching, hooked into the message.INT. MORNING KANSAS FARMHOUSE. ADELLE'S ROOM.PAN to ADELLE sleeping. The rooster crows out in the barnyard.ADELLETalking in her sleepRF - I can hear the voices - all the voicesRADIO (RELIGIOUS SHOW)And his face a radiance brighter than the sun, his eyes the deepest blue of the deep blue sea, his cloak and raiment the dazzling rainbow of multi-color light - he is coming back soon - he is coming back to us - yes he is - amen...EXT. VIDEO.VOWe want to give you a minute tothink about the saucer experience...The saucer in a field, larger than life...The hub door inches upward as light pours from the interior...a slope of long steps is revealed. ADELLEI hear all the stations - up here (points to her head) can't get some song out of my MIND - does that mean I'm out of my mind? It would take a village of the dammed to raise this child
MINI-MOVIE 7

OSCAR

I AM THE ONE

To:

Everyone -: I AM the One.

How do we have us versus them when we're all One?

ALIEN USHER

Your name?DAKWIllard - all night newsworker.ALIEN takes a pair of tickets.ALIENYou have two. We will bill your media establishment.DAKALIENAnd -- good luck.TEDDYWe got the tickets -- what's it mean, good luck?He turns to GWEN. She blinks her eyes at him like Morse-Code. HOPSITAL. HARLEM, NEW YORK CITY.CARL WASHINGTON as a boy, in the hospital.DOCTORHe can have the operation to relieve the pressure on his eyes. But he may not be able to see the little that he can now.MOTHER(crying)The Christmas tree lights.That's all he can see - he reaches out to them. It's his happiest day of the year.LITTLE BLACK BOY (CARL WASHINGTON JR.)Wears wrap around dark glasses.A vacant lot, debris - 360 pan dissolves to STONEHENGE.
MOCK DIRVISH re-enacters move around the stones, establishing a CONFIGURATION which emulates the arrangement of stars in the Pleaides Cluster. ARENA-SIZED AUDIENCE ENCOUNTER THEATER, like a planetarium, sports arena and Collesium -like encounter stage area, waiting. DAK WILLARDWhat do you get when you combine Pirandello and Fernand Lamaze?RODNEYWhat?DAKSix characters in search of an easy childbirth.

RODNEYJeez! Look at that. They've got a parking lot!ALONYea, wonder if they have ALIEN VALETS?
THE AUDIENCE files in, guided by alien USHERS.Sweeping camera moves cover the AUDIENCE taking their seats - the MARKEE displays word-phrases while sound accompanies"There is a tide in the affairs of men, which, taken at its full, leads on to great rewards -""The evil men do lives after them, while the good is oft interred with their bones..."Smiling happy-face ALIEN ICON floats over the audience. 3D notes floating burst and music plays in bursts.ADELLEI can be a MEDIA MAVEN! A goddess! I can sing & sing & sing just like a mob buy in a prosecution sentence deal. I can go beyond Karaoke! I can be a Jewel in the Mound of Venus! No answer. Oh well, this is an election year.

INTERIOR. PRESS CONFERENCE AREA. PEORIA.

An impromptu press conference setup in the cavernous building, set up like a political convention, cordoned off into sections.
Fleur-de-lis bas-relief on the back of the chairs.MCARE YOU READY? The aliens are about to appear.OSCAR, the ALIEN MASTER MAGICIAN, enters. He wears a dressing robe, and a belt which carries many devices. A glowing amulet around his neck. He has long hair and conveys the overall impression of a strange rock musician. A loin-purse gleams with a mutli-color diffraction grating.NOTE: A mixture (at various times) of Uncle Miltie, Werner Erhard, The Prince of Denmark, The Artist Again Known As Prince, Elvis (thin and fat), Mick Jagger, Jesus & a shaman, plus the Dark Prince, Ol' Scratch (Lucifer).Ground fog clings to the ground behind his feet, spreading, as though his passing has created condensation or a temporary change in the room's atmosphere.
OSCAR takes his seat in the center of a long table, surrounded by other aliens, the ASSISTANTS. The tableau is the setup of the Last Supper, OSCAR and twelve alien "desciples." OSCAR brushes his hair back, prepares to speak as boom mikes, tape recorders, light meters are thrust toward his face.
MARONG STEWART, the "betrayer" is at the end, like Judas Iscariot. In this guise he looks like one of the alien
Let's set up the theatrical

We have the physical avatars - the "costumes" in a trunk -

World media network - the "theater" of life - we are all actors - no?

A whole armada of alien saucer-theaters - WOW!

OSCAR
Can we compress the standard dramatic structure onto the progression of an Evolution Workshop?

ELDER
We have tickets to sell - do what it takes

OSCAR

Their most prolific playwright - wrote over 500 plays...Lope de Vega - lile my last name, the star my fam is from - upstaged by a Bill Shakespeare - he was given credit in Hollywood for over two hundred plays - most plagiarized from the central processor of the galaxy -

underlings.

RODNEY and ALTON follow the INTERVIEWER in for the close-up.Reporters start firing questions. The replies are cheeky, quick.

INTERVIEWER
What is your mission here?

OSCAR
To sell tickets. Create ticket VALUE

INTERVIEWER
How many can come to the Show?OSCARAs many as we can get in the door.

KIDS titter. Parents shush them.

OSCARNo standing room, though. Just enough to transform.

BARRY
What's he mean transform?

SHIELAShhh. Listen.

INTERVIEWERWhat is the content -- the message?OSCARThe message is the medium, it cannot bedescribed. Are you coming to The Show?

INTERVI EWER
I don't know it I have the time or the money.OSCARYou have both. There is enough time and enoughmoney in the world to see The Show. See you there.

INTERVIEWER
What is the means of propulsion of the saucers?

OSCAR
Fear.

INTERVIEWER
Fear of what?

OSCAR
Of staying in the same place.(laughter)

INTERVIEWER
How do you see the earth.

OSCARThrough the view port. (laughs)

INTERVIEWERAre we your equals, except for the

technology, or do you see us as children?OSCARAge is relative.INTCan you elaborate?OSCARWe are like the man whobuys a big house but then has a large mortgage. You are very charming.Like children, you arestill growing.INTERVIEWERIs that meant to be patronizing?OSCARNot yet.INTERVIEWERDo you believe in anything?OSCARWe believe in wherever we are. No belief required for The Show. It is so-called. That is the best name for what we do. There is no mystery. You knoweverything there is to know.What responsibility do you assumeMANWhat about the safety of the audience?OSCARYou all sign a waiver and release when you buy your tickets. There is no danger. OSCARWe will be holding a Saucer Lottery to determine who among you get to come to the show.

SAUCER LOTTERY

Line up for the Saucer Lottery
Take you number at the door
As you wait to get in
Can you hang onto it any more?
And it's 1, 1-2-1, 1-3-1
And the numbers of the saucers to be counted
The zero and the one connote a connection to someone...

SmartScreen DISPLAY:

OSCAR
You all will be entered into a saucer lottery, to see who will get the final seats.

SmartTV: SAUCER LOTTERY

VO: You all will be entered into a saucer lottery, to see who will get the final seats.Bioenergetics!

THE CELL MAGNET
Cellular Memory - Mixed with Audience Response

CLOSE Newspaper with the headline: UFOS A THOUSAND OF 'EM.SAUCERS HUNDRED SHARE (VARIETY)SAUCERS SELL OUT (NY/LA TIMES)SUPERMARKET SATURATION SUITS SAUCERS

EXT. DAY SAUCER -

THE PARKING AREA.
Disneyland-like, there is parking for 10,000 cars.

Cars move up to the ticket booths.

TEDDY

How much is it to park?

ALIEN$50

TEDDY
$50! I already PAID $500 for a ticket to get into this Show-thing.

ALIEN stares.

ALIEN
It's all abundance.

TEDDY
I'm the PRESS.

ALIENBuy a parking ticket too.TEDDYIt's not a "parking ticket" - that's if you DON'T pay - oh, you wouldn't know - you're not from here - can't use city parking for your ship anyway - oh ALL RIGHT - here's your FIFTY DOLLARS!

GWENHe just wants to park you.TEDDYIs this valet?ALIENNo man is a hero to his valet. Self parking only. So park yourSelf. If this were the LA saucer, we'd park you in the Val-ley!TEDDY (DRIVING)A wise ass. Shakespeare or something. Jeeez!GWENOh Teddy.EXT. NIGHT. THE SAUCER.10,000 people move from the parking lot to the saucer, like lemmings to the sea, rats to the Pied Piper.EXT. NIGHT. THE ALIEN MIDWAYALIEN HAWKERSBARRYHey look at this!ALIEN hands him a photo - his face appears as in a photograph - BARRYHow much?ALIENFifty dollars.BARRYFifty dollars -ALIENWhat you feel.BARRYHere's $20.Hands him a note. ALIEN leaves. Picture loses 2/3s of its image.BARRYHey come back - I WANT MY MONEY BACK!
STUDIO-MARONG STEWART
FOSS
We've found that the saucer spots are tightly controlled, run in a series for cumulative effect, and use subliminal cues plus some variations of image manipulation which are indecipherable.The technology is - alien. The image message is, apparently absorbed into the bloodstream through the eyes.Like a method of, reverse iridology,specific memory and body center.We have evidence to show the images hit as deepas the genetic cellular code.Yes - anyone who has seen the spot has experienced pre-set comparability with the desire to be drawn to the Show.They're going for 2% of the total world population.That's what it takes to get transformation.

SUPER ON SCREEN: PROGRAM OF THE SAUCER

GRAPH shows the major population density centers of the earth. A counter shows the world population.

EXT. THE GLEN OAKS PARK - DAYSAUCER FLOODLIGHTS bear down, Illuminating the surroundings

Tired-looking" GROUNDIES" set up the area around preparing the "alien midway" the saucer, set by set, an entire "midway town" appears around the saucer.
INT. THE SAUCER - DAYOSCAR LOOKS out of the HubBUB, scanning the horizon.ASSISTANT approaches.
WORKERDo you want the clones readied?OSCARYes, for tonight's presentation.EXT. NIGHT. THE SAUCER - OUTSIDE THE MAIN DOOR.The 10,000 AUDIENCE PARTICIPANTS stand lined up, ready to go in.The DOOR BEGINS TO RISE*KEY QUOTE SCENE - TRANSITION*Bright light emanates. Silhouette of aliens figures. Ten of them, descending a slight ramp, toward the crowd. Simultaneous, a row of TICKET BOOTHS rise out of the ground, as the aliens move forward. The lights dim. Detail of the uniforms is seen - like USHER uniforms.THE ALIENS take their places at the ticket booths, ready to scan the audience's tickets.ALIEN USHERS appear, at a long toll booth configuration, velveteen ropes, purple, uniform jackets with epaulets, stock alien "leotard" legs.The AUDIENCE moves forward.INT. DAY. THE SAUCER "FOYER"AUDIENCE moves forward, into the foyer-"lobby" - then up long 3-storey escalators - to the perimeter corridor around the saucer interior - the "corrimeter"AUDIENCE FACES are digitzed as they move past the booths into the foyer.ALIEN TRAVEL POSTERS on either side of the rising AUDIENCE heading for the circular interim areaTHE ESCARAMPSAs they rise, there are glowing rectangles on either wall - the display screens. On one side, there is an alien travelogue, moving pictures of landscapes on other planets. On the other side, the development of Man, from the simian form to present day is displayed in a series, leading up to the broad openings in the floor of the corrimeter which allow access from the escaramps. In other words, development up to today...and then the corrimeter which leads to the Theater of Evolution.INT. THE CORRIMETER - DAYPeople mill about, looking over the futuristic displays of alien technology - the corrimeter has the feeling of a trade show in a large hotel. Video screens project alien vistas. There are banks of telephones, automatic teller machines hooked into the major banking networks, there are alien-tech devices and demonstrations, food counters, bars, tables and chairs.Gliding small vehicles carry USHERS back and forth in the corridor.
\
Signs:EVERYTHING YOU WANT!INT. NIGHT. THE SAUCER.FLASHING LIGHTS in succession of three's. Signs flash, suspended in mid air THE SHOW IS ABOUT TO BEGINTHE AUDIENCE files in, guided by alien USHERS.It is hard to tell in the murky, stagey light just how large the saucer interior is. (Actually about the size of the superdome) The seating besides being variable-raked is staggered-low density, so that the seat TWO rows back looks over the seat in front.IThere are narrow aisles between the rows of seats. There is a conveyor surface which rins around IN FRONT of the SUPER-seats. At each end of these arcs of surface, there is a hemispherical grating device at the ends, which is used later to incorporate-discorporate objects circling and passing from one section to another.INT. THE SAUCER THEATER - DAYIt is impossible to tell just how large the interior theater is -- it is immenseNOTE: Actual dimensions are 250' high at the center, central stage 100' with "Exchange Seats" filling up the rest of the full 300' diameter of the central stage diameter. The total inner theater area is 1,000 feet in diameter.GWEN and TEDDY walk down the aisle, shown the way by an alien USHER. They take their seats, which are numbered and coded.There is a

general hubub as on opening night at a play. Authence members take their seats.THE SUPERSEATS: These are low-density seating, which means they take up a lot more space than normal theater seats. In fact, they are "staggered" so that on a low sloping incline, the line of sight is over the seat TWO rows ahead,Each seat is flanked by panels on either side.Like acceleration couches for astronauts. A surrounding headrest holds side speakers, and there is a clear globe over each seat, practically like a hairdryer arrangement, except that the bowls have a microphone attatchmnent. Images can be projected directly onto the globes helmet surface, or the helmets can selectively enlarge elements in the field of view, up to and including all portions of action on the stage.

(*NOTE: SUPERSEATS ARE GROUPED IN AN "EXCHANGE WEDGE," ONE OF TWELVE "POINTS" AROUND THE STAGE, 111 EXCHANGE SEATS PER WEDGE FOR A TOTAL OF 1332 EXCHANGE SEATS IN ALL.)TEDDY gingerly takes his seat. He squirms as the head globe descends over his face, and he has an (POV shot) enlarged, focussed view of the stage.Within the head globe visual displays are three sub-screens. One is bio-rythm, another heart rate and respiration,

another a "detail" screen. Plus there are two eyepieces, or goggles, which fit over the eyes.TEDDY takes the seat speaker, twists it toward his mouth. BARRY speaks into his seat speaker.BARRYI used to be in radio beforeSHIELAOh, Barry.BARRYI did sales, honey. I know all about it.SHIELAYou think you know everything.TEDDY sits in his seat. He is uneasy. TEDDY is not the kind of person who likes to give up his control of situations, and this is beginning to look like more than he had expected.ANGLE from just behind TEDDY's head, through the globe apparatus of the seat. He pulls down the globe.CLOSEfrom inside the helmet, we see the stage and its substages enlarged in the view. Projections of information on the sides present status of audience member, Show Act and personal biorythmn.TEDDY watches the stage.The lights of the saucer flash three times on and off, then begin a slow dimming.A Broadway-style musical fanfare, introduction of musical themes.DISSOLVE TOADELLE stands there watching, the lights playing on her face AS:The camera Point of View (POV) pulls back and cranes up to an overhead view of the area/ ADELE stands near the intersection of two roads, the CROSS of SPACE and TIME

JESUS Christ conquers l (IN OLD TEXT) The CROSS of space & time in the center of the SAUCEr - the blazing sun seen BEHIND the criss-cross.

INT. SAUCER. DAY/EVENING.

The CROSS OF ROADS changes color as the viewpoint pulls back.This dissolves into the saucer interior.P

ull back from stage center to the top of the CENTRAL CONSOLE in the saucer, showing the stage and the aisles, the STAGECROSS and the SUPERSEAT WEDGES

INTERIORThe Central Console lights up:THE SHOW IS ABOUT TO BEGINsimultaneous with their singing. The alien kids bow and scamper back to the wings under the SuperSeats.

INT. THE SAUCER - DAYCLOSE, the CENTRAL CONSOLE, CENTRAL MECHANISM, and the CELL MAGNET (retracted to its base)Lights GLOW from the central lighting grid -- brightly, piercinglyLOUD SYNTHESIZED TRUMPET SOUND: #$%&. Helmet interiors flash bright spectrum of colors. Multi-colored birds fly around the saucer interior, flocking and veering, going over the audience in great numbers and colors.ANNOUNCER'S VOICEGOOD EVENING LADIES AND GENTLEMEN AND WELCOME TO THE SHOW!

Central console (group of display screens like a hockey scoreboard)

OSCAR
I am the One. You're all One. Let's get you connected - in the right way.

Electronic images - movie like a rock n roll concert with aliens -

A huge DOVE flaps its wings above the audience, looking down, an olive branch in its beak

BARRY
Hey, look at that!

BILL
Don't drop on me.The lights flash and fade quickly.

Spotlight center stage.The stage is set at the 300' diameter, large as a football field. The audience of 8,000 in their superseats looks on.

SFX: FANFAREA video-processed announcer speaks from the overhead console.

ANNOUNCER

And now, ladies and gentlemen, here's the Count.. .one, two, three!

A LARGE BAND OF MUSICIANS, an alien orchestra, revolves 180 degrees from under the stage, fully set up, musicians alread in place, as they accomplish the incredible weightless turn, already playing. COUNT BINARY plays a huge gleaming piano, as he and the orchestra revolve up from below stage level.

COUNT BINARY, still pounding out a swing rythm, grins and plays as the stage spins around now, a stage sphere.. .turning like a musical bubble...The central display console, above the heads of the audience, flashes:

COUNT BINARY AND THE BLACK HOLE ORCHESTRATHE ALIEN ORCHESTRA rises in the stage sphere, shimmering.

FRANK SYMMETRY

a tall, gangling crooner from Zircon, descends from the overhead console on a beam of light.

Alien DANCERS emerge from the "wings" under the seating area anddance across the Parchisi-cross of the central stage. Their dance steps echoe like drumbeats.

The ORCHESTRA plays an alien swing tune. The musicians, all different aliens, writhe and shake to the music, playing strange instruments.

The musicians, all different aliens, writhe and shake to the music, playing strange instruments. The saucer rocks, the Count shaking, gyrating and grooving. The band seems to expand with their music, playing to burst.The music becomes faster and faster reaching an incredible "rave up" pitch - then finally ORCHESTRA visually implodes on the blast of a last trumpet and vanishes in a bright FLASH on the last note.

EXT. DAY. PEORIA LANDING SITE.A tent with a flapping "galactic" flag"

ALIEN JAMBOREE

The circus is in townThe saucer circle going 'roundI love you, you love THEMIt could all happen againShe was lost in the saucerOn a foggy foggy nightShe wasn't doin', she wasn't doin'It wasn't RIGHTOverdrive...OSCAR came to herYou're beautiful I seeMy husband doesn't appreicate meWell that may beThe saucer's a BOATSo don;t upset itIt can all happen - if you let itOhno noo no no - it;s not HalloweenIt's not something that you may have senThey're all in greenface and they're coming to your spaceIt's the alien jamboreee, and it;s for freeCome along with meCome along with me -

The DOOR BEGINS TO RISE

Bright light emanates. Silhouette of aliens figures. Ten of them, descending a slight ramp, toward the crowd. Simultaneous, a row of TICKET BOOTHS rise out of the ground, as the aliens move forward. The lights dim. Detail of the uniforms is seen - like USHER uniforms.

THE ALIENS take their places at the ticket booths, ready to scan the audience's tickets.

ALIEN USHERS appear, at a long toll booth configuration, velveteen ropes, purple, uniform jackets with epaulets, stock alien "leotard" legs.

AUDIENCE moves forward, into the foyer-"lobby" - then up long 3-storey escalators - to the perimeter corridor around the saucer interior - the "corrimeter"

Scrap of paper theory of information technology =

AUDIENCE FACES are digitzed as they move past the booths into the foyer.

ALIEN TRAVEL POSTERS on either side of the rising AUDIENCE heading for
the circular interim area
EXT. DAY – ADELLE

The TRUCK moves up to the intersection. A piece of paper flies up into the
air in front of the truck – ADELLE grabs at it through the window, gets it,
then loses it.

CLOSE – the paper through the air –

ADELLE grabs the paper, out of the truck now – it slips along the street, she
gets it and opens it – the PAPER is covered with heirogloyphics and
equations –

ADELLE
Hydroglyphics – what's it mean? Written in water?

"What's up, earth bro'. Are you trying to go onto the world level by "If that's
what you want to call it. Let's say that the saucers opened me up to new
purpose, at least by tangential contact.

INT. THE SAUCER – NIGHT.

JUMPING, JIVING ALIEN SWING BAND
plays on a revolving stage that revolves around from the stage floor level, so
the musicians who are upside down swivel to rightside up while the song is
played.

COUNT BINARY revolves up with the band already playing in the "upside
down" position. He is smiling at all the audience, his white teeth gleaming.

`You don't have to be the one to cry
You don't have to be the one to die...
There is a reason to your sensual season
There is a reason to your sexual season
It will be coming by and by...Travelin to planets at the speed of thought
This universe is the only one we got
There is a reason for your sensual season
There is a reason for your saucer seasonIt will be coming by and
by...(etc.)1-2-3-4-WHY -- Song of the Aliens
Band pumping out a skat melody, Zydeco.
You don't have to be the one to cryYou don't have to be the one to
die...There is a reason to your sensual seasonThere is a reason to your
sexual seasonIt will be coming by and by...Travelin to planets at the speed
of thoughtThis universe is the only one we gotThere is a reason for your

sensual seasonThere is a reason for your saucer seasonIt will be coming by and by...(etc.)

FANFARE
OSCARGOOD EVENING LADIES AND GENTLEMEN AND WELCOME TO THE SHOW!

Virtual butterflies leap out of the descending column.OSCARAND NOW ON WITH THE SHOW!CUT TOLOW SHOT - OVERHEAD - The Cell Magnet on BoomOSCAR above, on the CELL MAGNET, like a huge phallus between his legs. He demonstrates its extension-retraction capabilities. It should be overtly sexual.OSCARMade to melt in your mouth not in your hands - Mars needs women!
AUDIENCE: Big laughter track.CUTHe is at the CENTRAL CONSOLE, pointing out to the CELL MAGNET which begins to revolve.OSCARPay attention to this device.
THE CELL MAGNET comes to life, revolving on its boom, shooting out laser-like lights, glowing with sentience.The AUDIENCE bursts into titters and giggles.OSCARIt's tickling you.The CELL MAGNET revolves again. Groans of aches and pains are heard.Various outpourings of emotive exhortations.The CELL MAGNET dims. APPLAUSE signs flash around the stage. The audience applauds.DETAIL ON: "hairdryer" apparatus seats.CUTOSCAR is now down among the seats, the HAIRDRYER HEADGLOBE seats, walking along, looking at his audience members like a doting parent or salon owner.

A large flower BULB - the petals of the lotus blossom, begin to open downward - a column rises out of the middle.

CRASHING SOUND OF ORCHESTRAL DISSONANCE. The lights brighten, then dim. Spotlights appear. OSCAR stands on the podium, on the stage apparatus, above the five "modular stages."

OSCAR points a laser-light pen at the overhead CELL MAGNET.

OSCAR
This will definitely invade your space. Your INNER space. Stir up the emotions

He shines the light in a circle around the audience envelopes.

OSCAR
It is there to help you achieve the proper emotional response.

CENTRAL CONSOLE

SAPPHO & ZAPPA

ELDER

They will be loaded into the flop spheres - their identity, personality, potential conflicts, personal and world scales.

USHERS move along the contrayor aisles, helping AUDIENCE members get accustomed to the seat controls. Seats go back, up, turn, light up with dials and monitors.This way, the Elders who run the Program of the Show can make their adjustments appropriately.

INT. SAUCER. DAY/EVENING.

A full 360 circular movement around the rising figure of OSCAR in a blue rhinestone-studded jacked surveying the audience as he spins - 10,000 earth people waiting for transformation

ELDER
He looks out over the minions - can he succeed in Transforming them?

ELDER 2They seem so lost, so willing.

The lights flash and sequence through permutations, then go blazing-bright.STAR SPOT ON OSCARTHE CELL MAGNETOSCARGOOD EVENING LADIES AND GENTLEMEN AND WELCOME TO THE SHOW!Virtual butterflies leap out of the descending column.AND NOW ON WITH THE SHOW!OSCAR points a laser-light pen at the overhead CELL MAGNET.
OSCARNow watch this device -Do you believe in cellular memory?In bio-energetics?Then watch and see:It is the Cell Magnet - a beamer, a creator, destroyer and - an audience - empathizer - it warms you up to the topics we will present.For now, let us start with a change of scenery - or costume I should say.CELL MAGNET sweeps the audience, this bunch of ill-dressed future strivers, who all become formally dressed, black tie, tux on the men, gowns & flowers/pendants on the women. They look around. Gasps of surprise and approval.THE JUPITER'SAUDIENCE reactions are intense, driven by the CELL MAGNET, which moves over their heads.AUDIENCEAhhhh!HUGE planet-like objects roll out onto the stage from the "wings" - the entrances under the raked seating of the seat wedges. DANIEL.
TEDDY quick-scans the stage. The dancers swirl.
TEDDYLet's get out of here.
GWEN
I've never been so infatuated.That alien is positively -- charismatic...You've never given me such pleasure
The USHERS return to their positions outside the doors.
TEDDY gets up from his seat and struggles to the aisle. Three USHERS spot him and walk toward him.

USHER
Yes, may we help?TEDDYI need to leave. Sick. Throw up.USHERYou cannot leave. Return to your seat.TEDDYGotta GO!USHERFOLLOW ME BACK TO YOUR SEAT.You are not due to be part of the SHOW yet.TEDDY struggles with the portal, getting it to open to allow him to leave.TEDDY

Let me go.USHERYou paid, you are part of the show - by choice. I will show you to your seat.

USHER takes TEDDY by the arm. TEDDY struggles, hits the USHER on the beak, runs toward the stage. A barrier stops him, invisible. He turns around and runs for the EXIT.ALIEN WIERDNESS - THE COMPLICATION (LOST IN THE SAUCER)INT. THE CENTRAL CONTROL MECHANISM - ABOVE THE MAIN THEATERTen ELDERS (ANGELS) sit around a circular table THE VIEW CIRCLE, observing the stage action below through a viewscreen which takes in the entire saucer. Light pointer on TEDDY.

ELDEROne of them is escaping.ELDER 2The Ushers will get him.THE SHOW mellows then, the players dissolving back to their seats. THE DOPPLER DANCERS disappear from stage.INT. THE THEATER AISLE - NIGHTTwo USHERS see him and chase after him. He runs for the escaramnp.ANGLE: ESCARAMPThey throw something at his feet -- a clear surface which fits under his feet. TEDDY skids on it like a skate board, rounding the corridor to the escararnp.TEDDY flies down the ramp toward the hub door, which is closing slowly. He escapes underneath the door as it closes down; the USHERS run into it headlong.INT. CORRIMETER - NIGHTTEDDY pushes through them to his car. EXITS are put on SAFETY to prevent others from escaping. The exit doors seal shut with an implosion of air. WHOOMP!ANOTHER ANGLEThe

DISENFRANCHISED, those who did not get into the SHOW because of no money, see him running, move forward to surround him.They grab at him, at his formal attire.

MANWhat was it like?
WOMAN
Is it anything like dying?
YOUNG MAN
Is it better than an acid trip?
TEDDY
What's an acid trip?
YOUNG MAN
We take it when we study the 1960'sin school! Is it better?
TEDDY
Let me out of here!

INT. SAUCER. NIGHT.Central Console display:
EXT. SAUCER PARKING. NIGHT.

The zombie-like DISENFRANCHISED crowd around the rear of the car, blocking his backing out.TEDDY honks, backing into them. They scatter. One indigent falls under the wheel.
INDIGENT
Owwww!TEDDYSorry! Sue me!He drives through the crowd, scattering them, burning out of the parking lot toward the main access road.

INT. THE STAGE - ANOTHER ANGLEOSCAR stage-center.
OSCAR
Everyone has a Saucer Name. As the boom revolves, speak your name to it.

The CELL MAGNET revolves. Hubub of sound as audience members speak their names.Interior, headset.

GWEN speaks her name into the mouthpiece.

OSCAR
Now, type your response.Why am I here?Who am I?

The third "panel" of superseats slaps across their laps. Those who can type begin clicking their response.DISSOLVE TO:INTERIOR HELMET: close view of stage.The SAUCER STAGE lights up like a huge game board, a TV game show.BARRY, SHIELA, FARO and FOSS move to the stage area.
They stand in a pit area like THE PRICE IS RIGHT.
(No

Central Console:
SAUCER SAYSSAUCER SAYS

They become pawns in a board game - LIFE-SIZE VALUE GAME

OSCARWhat is the value proposition -The prizes descend from the overhead ceiling plate, descending on yellowish gravity beams, objects touching down around the stage in sequence with the overhead console flashing prices in money systems throughout the galaxy.
OSCARHUMANS, COME ON DOWN!
AUDIENCE MEMBERS begin running for the stage.All sequences from original Price Is Right, digitally remastered to PLAYERS jump up onto the stage. A GAMEMASTER enters the stage arena.

THE AISLES around the stage become gridded, flashing bands of color.
OSCAR
Show us your Lark pack! Fight regressive Evolution with a checkup and a check. You have this dance of pro-creational potential –
You have us and the bio-paks you live with.

SWEEPING CAMERA MOVES -Smoke swirls. The STAGE spins as a large roulette wheel. THE Circle of Life - grab the Brass Ring.The audience members are jolted out of their seats to stand ready.GWEN SHIELA BARRY and FOSS stand as pawns.The GAMEMASTER uses an instrument like a cattle prod, on a smaller scale, to urge them to marked spots on the GAMEBOARD.BARRY runs up the ramp.
DISSOLVE TO:The saucer, divided into 12 main sections, lights up like a huge roulette wheel. The 60 degree sixth sections flash alternately with the twelve wedge section lights.CURRENCY SYMBOLS light up all around the saucer, DOLLAR SIGNS plus POUND SIGNS, FRANCS, LIRA, etc. Flashing like on a game show.OSCARYOU CAN HAVE ANYTHING YOU WANT!
The seat helmets (various) glow with astrological readouts, projections of biorhythms, personality matrix.

ASTROLOGICAL SYMBOLS appear on the inner wall of the theater perimeter. The overhead console flashes bright lights.The Superseats make the audience members look like they are under hair dryers. Row after row.

Onstage Parade: on the floating float: THE EARTH QUEENFOR THE DAY

INT. SAUCER. NIGHT
"QUEEN FOR A DAY" sequence.
GWEN is pulled out of the audience, draped with a robe & crownedwith a tiara.
She walks down the runway, back toward the audience

QUANTUM COSMOLOGY ONTOLOGY IT'S GOOD TO BE QUEEN

THE PAIN OF SEPARATION IS NO CUTE, IT'S ACUTE

It's about the money system - the filthy lucre - the dirty green -

GREEN IS GREEN - MONEY IS HONEY

INTERIOR. HEADGLOBE SCREENThere is a character printout:

CARL WASHINGTON
I am here wearing a green tie - the color of dead presidents - I want to MONEY - I am here to win the Saucer Dollars! My name is the same as the man on the bill, so if you will, and I will, I will take the MONEY!

The CELL MAGNET can make huge sweeping 360 degree turns just like the stylus on a CD player - the biotechnology is set up the same. It "reads" the audience bio-rhythms
THE GIMME SHOW FOR-U TOTAL DOMINATION OF WORLD MARKETS
With 3-VIEW coverage of the stage action of the GIMME SHOW.OSCAR rises on the GIMME SHOW set.OSCAR'S VOICEYou can win -- a NEW CAR!
The CELL MAGNET spins, JET-FAST, STOPPING AT FACES IN THE AUDIENCE.A NEW AMARSKID CAR descends on a gravity beam toward the stage, stopping several feet above the stage surface.CELL MAGNET stops on a dime on CARL:OSCARWhat do you say?CARLI WANT it!Jumping up and down, shaking his fists.CARLI WANT it!

FAST PAN TO:
BILL and MARTHA EVANS cheer, laugh, quiver, jump up and down, cry and laugh, shouting.

FAST PAN:REYNOLDS then ALTON, RODNEY then ADELLE, awe--struck.Some audience members, overcome, begin sobbing and retching, gagging on happiness.OSCARYou can have EVERYTHING YOU WANT!SHOCK PAN CUTS:
ANGLESA world's worth of products begin descending on wires (or gravity beams) to the stage.Women and men begin crawling to the stage perimeter, like the crippled at a healing revival meeting. BEAMS of light surround them,

healing, glowing.OSCARIf you reach the stage, YOU CAN HAVE - !HASSA new washer, three pump, three speed wash!OSCAREverything you want!

PRICE IS RIGHTCOME ON DOWN COME ON DOWN

Turns into Jeux San Frontiers game setup, within Parchissi, within Price is Right

OSCAR
Deus Ex Machina

OSCAR
You take the best of the Rave
Put your past in the grave
Start out with new skin

CENTRAL CONSOLE: "WELCOME TO EARTH – NO WAIT FOR WEIGHT"

People are straining to be in the fifth dimensional realm – our thought forms what we choose – our seNse of ourselves as the infinite -

INT. NIGHT. PEORIA BLACKLIGHT BAR.

OSCAR
Time is shrinking – all these ways of getting there to the end of time the end of space and the universe -

WORKSHOP configuration, Presenter (alien) Audience (Earthlings)

OSCAR
You will get to the end of your lives. The question is: in what condition?

It will get better because it HAS to, otherwise you aren't around to worry about it.

Sign on the T-Shirt
CHANGE I can believe in

Like Kris Angel – I am your angel, baby, for your planetary startup AND for your advice and lovelorn pages – a showman

GO out and have a good life – that's an order – we ARE the best ad and branding campaign since Jesus and the Bibles. Remember that group?

The idea is: to get you all connected.

ON STAGE

BARRY runs through the GAMES WITHOUT BOUNDS stage set. There is a spiral rampway, leading up to the top of the money pyramid. There, a large eye balefully regards the players. It is the currency pyramid.

OSCAR appears at the top, on the platform, next to the large eye. He points to BARRY.

OSCAR
Illuminati! Go to the end of the hall
There's the Council of Foreign Relations – 666 for ALL!
"Connection without conformity
Don't rely on global economy."
We are aliens, encounter us all

OSCAR
Where are you going?
BARRYI don't know. I'm here.
OSCAR
Where would you like to go?BARRYTo the top. To the very very top.
OSCAR
THEN YOU WILL GET THERE!Before you were not interested. Now you are interested.
BARRY runs.
THE MATRIX SPINS, the circular stage.
BARRY
How can I gain advantage here. Come out ahead of the other guy.

OSCAR
We are ready to Transport your Entire planet to the nearest Safe Planet Haven - what you may have called The Rapture, Reincarnation, the Ascention, whatever your ultimate cosmology calls for.

OSCAR
You cannot come out ahead of the other guy.You can only win through surrender. There IS not getting ahead or taking advantage – we are all One & we are all CONNECTED

BARRY
That was my training.

OSCAR
Forget all previous associations.
The best thing about association is that it is free.

EXT. TEDDY'S HOUSE - NIGHT

TEDDY burns up the street, screeching across his own lawn, upsetting the ABS display on his lawn which goes slicing through a fire hydrant. Water gushes up into the air.
TEDDY parks, in the driveway, gets out, looks at it. TEDDY shakes his head.
TEDDY
Now – that's ALIEN!

TEDDY runs for the garage and inside.
INT. TEDDY'S HOUSE - NIGHT
TEDDY leans against the wall of his porch, panting, breathing heavily. He pulls himself together and heads into the kitchen.OSCAR is seated there, at the table. There is another ABS board standing in the kitchen, behind OSCAR.

OSCAR
YOU are the alien. I'm just The Show. You could be the Show-Stopper. The Show must go on.
The walls drop away, we see layering of the master saucer. Like the living diagram. OSCAR leads TEDDY over to it.

OSCAR
All around the Saucer.

SAUCER STAGES
Fast fast fast...E stands for Everything
You have run but you have not gone far - why is that?
Look, is it something personal or why can't you aliens just leave us ALONE
Because I am what you might call the author, the author of The Show.
The author? Well, you better go back to Vega
Get some writing lessons, buddy
Skulls sinking into
Not everyone saw what you saw.
What - are you trying to say I was seeing things?
That it was ME making those obscene PICTURES?
It always takes two to make a Show - actually
One to one in many - yea.She was waiting on the road for he demon loverShe was a maiden oh so bold, but she had never know a suitorThe KudaliniHatha hatha hatha karma on little darlin'It's just a dangerous situationGetting back to basics, getting back to basicsResting on laurels

DISSOLVE as he speaks the words, from TEDDY's to

INT. SAUCER - ON STAGE

OSCAR
(Mouthing-shouting
YOU CAN HAVE EVERYTHING YOU WANTEVERYTHING YOU WANTEVERYTHING YOU WANT

INT. SAUCER. OSCAR faces the audience

OSCAR

YOU are the aliens, and we LOVE you don't you GET IT?

CONTACT YOURSELVES!

The Kudalini
Hatha hatha hatha karma on little darlin'
It's just a dangerous situation
Getting back to basics, getting back to basics
Resting on laurels
YOU CAN HAVE EVERYTHING YOU WANT
EVERYTHING YOU WANT
EVERYTHING YOU WANT
YOU CAN HAVE EVERYTHING YOU WANT!

OSCAR

YOU CAN HAVE EVERYTHING YOU WANT

TEDDYYea? I want out. I want you to leave.

OSCAR
Except that.

TEDDY
That's not very original - going there was like a cult, like sinning - nothing
new there. Whoever said sin was that original?

Just old New Age - It's the old bag of crapola.

Follow us and we'll lead you somewhere - all THAT.

OSCAR
Where do you think you got those concepts. It takes- it always - takes two to
make The Show.

TEDDYYou should try talking to my wife sometime.

OSCARYOU should try it. Two could be: earth and saucers, ground and sky.
Don't ask me why.

TEDDY
No.

OSCAR

NO WHAT? THAT IS NOT A COMPLETE STATEMENT.

TEDDY
Try talking to my wife sometime.

OSCAR
You can -- in the saucer theater.

TEDDY
You say that quick - like a dog name. "SaucerTheater" like one run-on word.
It won't work. Gwen and I are through. I left her there.

OSCAR
So I can pick her up? She's still there.

TEDDY
Get out of MY HOUSE!

OSCAR
I am the ONE! You are the One.

TEDDY begins to scurry around the house.

Oscar
Everything falling apart?

TEDDY grabs a can from the table, where he is gathering food for the woods.
He hurls a can in OSCAR's direction.

OSCAR is drawn back into the ABS board, which disappears.

TEDDY looks out the window to where the FOUNT is still rising, pumping
water into the sky, a foreboding of the energy founts at the end of the script.

Cheshire Cat smile in the window pane, like a reflection: the ALIEN

SMILE
There is no such thing as an alien. We are all aliens.

DISSOLVE TO:

INT. NIGHT. THE SAUCER THEATER.CENTRAL CONSOLE:
LECTURE ON RELIGION

OSCAR appears Sinatra-Bowie like, cool, in appears, in trenchcoat, smoking
a cigarette. He walks across the water, puffing the cigarette, his dark glasses
obscure his face.He faces the audience.

OSCAR
(talking-singing)
Religion is the ultimate in unrequited love.

AUDIENCE BOOS
Little backup aliens scurry out onto the stage, joining into a cluster to
sing:(rapid fire)

Think of it. You've been praying - if you're a Christian - for two thousand years to the image of awho may have had some contact with the invisible being you're supposed to love.

OSCARIf you're not Christian, you may have been praying longer.AUDIENCE LAUGHTERSINGERSWhat's that love which is never there? Children die in their cribs,planes crash while taking off,volcanoes erupt, earthquakes andtornadoes destroy life.OSCARIs that love?Really people. Some of you haveeven thought that UFO's -- that's us-- were the Savior from Outer Space.

The SINGERS "OOOOOO"

OSCAR
Does that sound reasonable to you?For all your prayer and effort, isthat love of God that supposedly onthe receiving end of your frustrationsreally coming through for you?

SINGERSIs it helping you to shape yourexperience or to create yourfuture? Is that idea of love just anagreement between people who can'tfind anything better to do?LAUGHTERA slinky alien torch singer joins OSCAR under the spotlights.TORCH SINGERYou don't have to believe to be.You don't have to believe in me.OSCARThere is no fatalism.TORCH SINGERFate is the way you relate.OSCAR(normal voice)Does anybody here need that to be said again?SILENCE.

OSCAR reaches the last pool of spot light.OSCARAny questions?OSCAR takes his place as a podium rises out of the stage circlewhich he stands on. The circle rises, the spotlight following it.OSCAR

Questions?

CELL MAGNET POV on a man in his seat, his questions flasherblinking.MAN(through seatmike)But what about the morality of thecommunity? What about the workethic. And the other things that bind people together? How do youattain that without a higher spiritual power?OSCARThank you . That is a good question. By asking that question have you in any way shaken your religious beliefs?MAN(defiantly)NO1

OSCARThen I would say the power to choose your belief resides in you.Maybe we ARE your saviors from the sky. Is this your Armageddon? YourMillennium? Your Rapture? Have any or you Christians disappeared lately?

LAUGHTER
Anything which is experienced fully disappears. Maybe this is what wasmeant by your prophets. We may notbe your saviors. You may be OURsaviors.

SINGERSWhen you fully experience our message,then we will disappear, and you willfind your rapture - here.OSCARRelativistically speaking,anything could happen,and temporally, it probably already has.SILENCEEven now you see us as gods.Two thousand years ago you wouldhave perceived us as Gods Twothousand years ago, it is possibleyou DID perceive us as Gods.How would that sit with you?If we're at the root of your beliefsystems, and we're just a bunch oftricksters, pranksters,vaudevillians out for a lark, howwould you believe in your futures?Do you want to doubt your history?Should you give up religion becauseyou can doubt it?SONG "SOMEDAY A MAN WILL COME"Someday a man will comehe does and when he doesWe'll all think of what we haveAND WHAT we'll have because of himAnd when that Time Comes

OSCAR
On the other face of conflict is Love – on the other side of fight there is surrender -

SPOTLIGHT ON OSCAR
If you read scripture, you know there's a trip there...
If you believe!

ON STAGE CENTER

OSCAR
Am I that man? No belief needed. Do you want to give it?
What if: There is no such thing as an alien. We are all in this universe together.

YOU ARE NOW HOLDING THE UNIVERSE WITHIN YOU, AT THIS SECOND, AT THIS MOMENT.

The stage turns black, becomes a black hole, a vortex pulling thevisual elements of the saucer into a blur of shape.

OSCAR ponderously sinks into the water, out of sight.

INT. NIGHT. THE SAUCER THEATER.
OSCAR on stage with the BLACK HOLE ORCHORD GROUP
THEY fire up a heavy slide-guitar anthem, stylized for the earth audience.Five aliens on futuristic "space guitars"

OSCAR
But why change places when the only concern is death & destructionSex mixed with death in most minds are the nexus of Creation!It is the cross-fertilization, the mixing and the blendingThe exchangingOn the wings of lust comes our escape from DustWill you give it back?Will you give it back to the next generationOr hold onto it - the treasure is life -The stars are information , passion and desireIf you can't take the heat --GET OUT OF THE KITCHENSpace is cool, and the only thing that isThe process, the process is warm...Your heart is warm, the galaxy is warmYour mind is one with the universeAnd the universe is all oneAll the information in the Universe is

contained within...Stored until it explodes, and another knowledge-cluster is formedBut why change places when the only fear is death and destructionSex mixed with death in some minds is the nexus of creation, yea, yea, yea

INT. "NIGHT" - THE SAUCER INTERIOR.OSCAR turns his attention to the rest of the audience -- four-headed, he faces the four quadrants simultaneously, Krsna-like.OSCARHave a conversation with yourselves.
Pick a person you know, talk to them through you.

CLOSE SHOT: OSCAR

OSCAR:
HAVE A NICE DAY. THAT'S AN ORDER.

INT. MARONG STEWART HEADQUARTERS -- 1 INFINITE LOOP, CUPERTINO -- DAY.

PIRATE SCULLY
We cannot control the Brigade anymore.
CHAIR 2They have left the impact area and are headed for the Colorado Nexus.

PSCULLY
WE MUST TRACK THEM.

DISSOLVE

EXT. DAY. THE PLAINS OF WYOMING.

The BRIGADE head across the plains on their power steeds.Their Powersteeds move ponderously.

CLOSEUP
EGO and DR. SAX lead the BRIGADE.
EXTERIOR. THE WOODS.
TEDDY and OSCAR sit on either side of the Ring.
OSCARYou must get the Brigade.

THE RING - THE VIEWCIRCLE

The ring between them grows and becomes a viewport into the control area above the saucer theater. Their viewpoint merges with the viewport within the Control Room, and they are looking down at the audience in the saucer theater.

They look into the VIEWCIRCLE.

OSCAR spins a coin, it becomes a Sphere, pushing out light - dazzling to the eye, mesmerizing.

BIG SCREEN DISPLAY:

THE CRAZY MAN'S WAY TO RICHE$!

SAUCER DOLLARS
THE MONEY SYSTEM TAPE & TAPEWORM SET

INTRODUCING SAUCER DOLLARS!!!

Order your set NOW! $39.95

We will get into your money system, one way or another -

DETAIL: FULL SCREEN STAGE PHENOMENA.

"Event" pyramids appear at the edges of the hole. Audience members are drawn into the pyramids. Their bodies are warped and pulled visually and viscerally. GWEN appears as a Goddess-figure, within the pyramidic grid -

GWEN
For a long time, the Dolphin Starglyph just seemed to be an abstract form of geometry that didn't really seem to lead to an understanding, other than that which was obvious on the surface. When I found that same geometry within the third eye of the Chakra Formation, the Dolphin Starglyph became very understandable and also became for me, one of the more important Starglyphs to appear. The Dolphin Starglyph then opened the Chakra Starglyph's light of understanding so that it could pour into the waters of the Universe of our third eye. The symbology, as I knew and understood it, was reflecting the deeper ways of universal and self love. It expressed swimming into the waters of the Universe and reflecting the greatest light. If one looks at water when the sun is reflecting on water, it prisms the light into magical beams made of stars that reach into every direction. This is the essence of what we are gifted with when we are able to walk with these understandings as part of our everyday world.

DAZZLING EFFECTS. The event horizon, where material and spiritual planes meet -- the material/spiritual "sky" --

LIGHTS DIM. SOUNDING OF LARGE CLOCK, LIKE BIG BEN.

Background: The overhead plane disc of the theater ceiling becomes animated with detail of TIME, the SEAL OF THE SAUCER.

The ceiling plate becomes dotted with details of the numerology of the universe.

MINI MOVIE 8: A NUMBER'S GAME -

OSCARTHE WORLD STARTED AS NUMBERS. WE STARTEDAS NUMBERS. IT'S A NUMBER GAME, THIS UNIVERSE.

We travel by numbers; you stay by numbers.You are all accounts in the universal bank.Earth, your number is up. You areaccountable.The metronic system:2% of world population - based on 1280 saucers -
It is US versus YOUR WORLD

Dorsey & the Orchestra –

"IS THIS CONSCIOUSNESS
DID I BRING THIS MELTDOWN ON?
DID I CREATE THE OIL SPILL AM
I LEADING POLYANNA'S WHO I
WANT TO WOO-WOO WITH YOU..."

All those who know Universal Law cannot help and respond.

The SPOTLIGHT bears down on the podium, focusing. OSCAR puts on boxing gloves. Behind him, the stage is transformed into a boxing arena.

OSCAR
Yes, you sir! What is competition but disguised com-violence? Is it creative or destructive?

No matter how commercial, territory He shadow boxes, dancing around the stage. A PARTICIPANT stands. He shakes his fist.

PARTICIPANT
If life won't flow, you gotta push it!

The PARTICIPANT is launched into the stage arena. Opposite OSCAR; gloves appear on his hands.

OSCAR
Anyone else? Do you buy that? Put up your dukes, asshole.

Another PARTICIPANT rises. On the four stage substage rings, mud wrestling sexy alien dancers appear between the boxers, dance stepping through their punches.
PARTICIPANT 2There's too much violence. It comes from television and pornography and advertising. It's all too violent. Too lurid!
OSCARWhat should we do about it?The women and men struggle in the mud.BRANCA
What should we do with all the evil in the world?

Man
Shut it off it is killing us! Shut it off -

The sound of money

THE SOUND OF MONEY
Final confrontation between
good and evil in the form of the
Saucer Arenas and the Estate II
Multi-Nat Corp selling super-cheap
computers (like Microsoft and Apple combined)

Cash registers jingling, slot machine mellifluous tonality, the symphony of
risk and chance -

GAS begins to rise out of the holes in the stage grid. Respirators descend
from the overhead surface.

Silly human conflict - takes precedent over everything -

We waste so much time or energy getting

THE SAUCER SEASON: ULTIMATE ENCOUNTER

We can learn to create our OWN future. We don't HAVE to focus on the
afterlife - it will come if it is there, anyway. We need to get work done
HERE.The audience APPLAUDSMANOur own actions produce the change. It's
all so obvious.OSCARACTIONS SPEAK LOUDER THAN WORDS

TEDDY
All right - I'll go back on one condition. Leave my wife OUT OF THIS. Leave
us ALONE.

Spin-DISSOLVE back to the saucer interior.

We can't hand out Abundance to these people - they are hung up on

OSCAR
WE MUST

Watch my ass end

OSCAR
Watch their asccend

AROUND ON THE CARROUSEL

Don't go for my wife!

OSCAR
T

Watch out for the

OSCAR
Right, now let's have some lights and action.
CENTRAL CONSOLE SIGN:

OSCAR
Adelle Wheat, come on down!

MINI-MOVIE 9(compressed): the rags to riches story

ADELLE
I was born in a shack
Al I had was hanging on my back

ADELLE is launched into the game matrix from her seat. She is caught into the matrix and lowered onto the stage.OSCARSignificant failure: what I am is not enough.

ADELLE is on the Gameboard Spot. Tied like spider web

OSCAR
Conclusion: do anything to gain approval. Create your act.
Adelle, who kept you from doing what you wanted to?

ADELLE
I did. It was my fault.

OSCAR
All right, what do you want to do now?

ADELLE
Be happy, become a better person.

OSCARHow's your sex life?

ADELLE
I have transcended sex.

OSCAR
What? You have transcended sex, the ROOT of community? How is that?

ADELLE
I have -- other things more important.Better things to do with my time.

OSCARAND YET -- that is what you think about the most.You NEED the contact with the

ADELLENo -- not that. Romance. Good feelings. Not
the crudity of sex.
OSCARSex is not crude ---- only your attitude toward it. We are each -- all of
us -- a product of it.We are each a fuck that got through. We pretty it up
with a lot of talk about the "blessed event but without some juice it would
not happen

 ADELLE
I -- I know -- but --guys always know what they want first.

OSCAR
Strip for us.
ADELLEWhat?
OSCAR
Do a dance. You are the sexiest person in the world. Show us -- do a dance
and make a show of taking off your clothes as you dance.

ADELLE blushes. The CELL MAGNET stops over her. She takes her skirt off
and throws it toward the audience.

ADELLEKansas City Star!
OSCARThat's what you are. Star that you are.

OSCAR

The men in the audience cheer.

ADELLE does a bumping, grinding strip, to great applause from the
AUDIENCE.

OSCAR
We're all from the stars. Be the star that you are.

TEDDY is lifted up and thrown into the saucer-matrix.TEDDY lands back at
the DOOR to the corrimeter, runs through it as it attempts to pucker and
close.A large SPRING launches TEDDY up into the CELL MAGNET matrix - a
BEAM traps TEDDY and flings him to the stage. ADELLE is entering the door,
late, being escorted by an USHER.

The CELL MAGNET lifts her skirt, then her, up into the air.

A Trapeze appears. She grabs it, heads down toward where TEDDY is flying
through the air, then he grabs a trapeze and they head toward each other.
She does a flip off the trapeze and lands in his arms, he lifts her and they
kiss.

OSCAR as the RINGMASTER applauds their union.

We can offer them Abundance

They wouldn't know what to do with it - we like to keep them enslaved in the System

They believe in it with a faith stronger than in God - and that's us - religio nis magic, and magic is technology -

In the magical infinitude of All - we soar above the heads in a balance

ADELLE and TEDDY meet a la TRAPEZE (Burt Lanchaster & Gina Lolabrigida) in TRAPEZE

TEDDY
Do you come here often? Nice to meet you in mid air!

TEDDY flips through the permutations, ADELLE lands in a safety net after letting go.

OSCAR
We're all from the stars. Be the Star that you Are

APPLAUSE

DISSOLVE TO:

OSCAR
Welcome back all my people, so ready to evolve.

EXT. DAY. THE GROVE.

FOR THOSE WHO ARE ABOUT TO EVOLVE

TEDDY
What exactly does evolution mean?

The Grove IS A MAGICAL PLACE. Around, there are Bliss Lights - Teddy crouches in the star field of blue lights.

The spinning bicycle, the bike on its side in the clearing, TEDDY running, background.

DISSOLVE TO: THE GROVE
Background element: A wide swath of stars - the Milky Way across the sky

Interior saucer (the spinning wheel becomes the spinning interior of the saucer, PARTICIPANTS skating through the ROLLER DERBY stage-set)The saucer spins, creating G-forces for the audience. DETAIL SHOTS: the audience showing 3-5 G facial distortion, grimaces. The saucer spins slows down.

Oscar

The stars are magic.

TEDDY
Yea, very nice.

OSCAR
No I mean they are really magic - we create them and sometimes they
disappear. YOU create them every time you look at them.

CENTRAL CONSOLE: EMOTIONS

Cell Magnet POV stops on FARO CONSTATINOPLE.

FARO
OSCARWhy do you avoid what you can do

SONG: "TOO LATE FOR LOVE"

MINI MOVIE 8 – THE SHOW PROGRESSES – EST TO ENCOUNTER

OSCAR
EST mean "to be" - Ontolo-GEE.

OSCAR
Fight regressive evolution with a checkup and a check – RISE above your
money system – that is Rise Up above your filthy lucre – above your two
cent's worth – rise above your mortgage, rise above the status at birth -

Yes, Virginia, there is a saucer - Pop my white owl cherry in the proper
fashion FOR the world?

FARO
I don't know.

OSCAR
You can do so much good - why are you so evil?

FARO
I can use my vision to achieve power. I can get what I want.

CELL MAGNET shows CLOSEUPS of audience faces.

OSCAR
Share.

DISSOLVE TO:

BIFF
What's this? human potential?

OSCAR

It's whatever you say it is.

DAK reaches out to his typewriter – touching it, it takes him on a TRIP

If I say it is write, it is written. I say.

Don't write what I write, write what I tell you to write - you are channeling
this- Got It?

OSCAR
Perhaps - it goes beyond you ability to write?

DAY INTO NIGHT (ROAR OF THE UNIVERSE)

For the Next stage of evolution I'll stay here
I'm not ready' No no
You weren't ready
You cannot make him come back - he must make the choice - he must
choose
It is no good for us to do it FOR you, you must do it for yourselves.

TEDDY projected from OSCAR's beam, descends from the overhead console,
flying through the air.

A TRAPEZE rises to meet his outstretched arms. He SWINGS past ADELLE
sweeping her into the air.Their FACES, close.

TEDDYYou're what I need you to be my first lady. Together, we'll run.

INT. THE SAUCER.
The central stage is an old railroad roundhouse depot.
LARGE CHUGGING SOUND like a large steam locomotive.

ADELLE is tied to the tracks. OSCAR appears, the evil monger. He snickers
and pulls at his moustache as the TRAIN approaches, huge clouds of steam,
bearing down.THE JAWS OF DEATH appear on the stage matrix. JAWS OF
DEATH becomes the WHEEL OF FORTUNE.
Double turning wheels with teeth and fire, spinning, threatening to crush
anyone who comes near. There is money in balloons, flying through a
cyclone, inside the jaws.

TECH CARNIVAL - HUMAN ZOO -

OSCAR
Here there be PIRATES

SHIELA walks out onto the gangplank of the stage-cross, toward the center
of the JAWS.

The saucer stage becomes transformed into an enormous CARROUSEL.
OSCAR rides on the inner horse, jumping off to run around the adult-
children.

The Game turns the players more and more into children, infants with
tantrums.They ride the MERRY GO ROUND which the stage becomes.

They grab at the BRASS RING.

BUSBY BERKELEY WEDDING CAKE MONEY SYSTEM SHOW-STOPPER

OSCAR(riding on the Hub)

Here under the Big Top - Grab the brass ring, everyone.
THE CAROUSEL OF LIFE takes over the saucer stage, spinning.Busby
Berkeley sacred geometry, fractal patterns

OSCAR
If you were a galactic race sending messages, and you on earth wanted to
receive them, forget about the radio waves – good for talk radio but nothing
as profound as the geometric display of the Crop Circles – they were your
Message in a Bottle from the Stars!

SFX: CALLIOPE MUSIC. 5-RING CIRCUS OF MYTHOLOGY AND EVOLUTION

The PARTICIPANTS become their animal look-alike, parading around the
central stage like "elephants on parade" -- Ringling Bros saucer stage.

What kind of animal will you become. Recycle? Go through the life pattern
again?

OSCAR
What's it all about Alfie?

Alien HANDLERS move with them.

The people become transformed, gradually, into animal figures. They take on
the look of animals but retain their human-like personality characteristics. A
swishy, sexy filly horse, tail snapping.

OSCAR
You are evolving from your animal selves, up through the genetic
evolutionary, creational chain, encompassing all that comes before, then
going to the next level - the universal oversoul -

They evolve back into themselves through the reverse shape-changing

OSCAR
Just as you did, we evolved into a money system. To the point where
everything had a price. Then we evolved beyond price. You must keep
evolving.

SONG: "SAUCER SEASON"

UFO's and cattleHere in the StarmanA levitated heifer, a communications satelliteSHOOTING STAR MANY TIMES MORE BRILLIANTBringing the cows home...It was big, Martha and me were sitting on the stoopI'm a hamburger, one of 18 multiple personalitiesMartha's my mother, yea...Hold things in the future, in the mind of the UniverseAnd the saucer and the egg, which came first?Three kids from LA, monetary gain was all the motiveBarley for Budweiser was better...A hundred windows light up like a markeeThe windows light up with all the faces...There is a time for Saucer Season...To every saucer there is a reason...

THE CAROUSEL now becomes a large vortex, and the AUDIENCE MEMBERS become roller derby hounds, skating down the centerline of gravity toward the pit, reaching for the baton, the brass ring, gleaming.
"SAUCER SEASON" The crystal amulet will show the WayThe crystal talisman transmutes time and spaceThe genetic change by the majesty of spaceShe's up in space in a Mothership...
THE BARNYARD PARTY ANIMALS.Kegs of beer roll out onto the stage.
USHERS put the kegs out, PBA's walk around the stage bellowing at each other.
INTERIOR. THE SAUCER.

CONTACT

CONSOLE: ACTS 5647-6897 "THE MANDALA OF ALL"

OVERHEAD VIEW of the entire saucer. SLOW ZOOM out Divided into the 12 pie-wedge sections.

TEDDY
Alien tricksters.

DELIVERY OF THE BEAST BY MICROBEAST

The central stage opens like an enormous eye, as the saucer- womb sac turns out baby MARONG STEWARTS (666 of them, each with a 666 on the forehead) which enter carrying ESTATE II computers for the Marketplace. BUSBY BERKELEY style musical a stack of cake tiers each a saucer -ALIEN dancers parade around in a circle -The GAMEBOARD of the saucer and begin their trip to the outer exits, corrimeter, and the world.
"SAUCER SEASON" (CONTINUED)The Dali Llama was in the Ashtar CommandNow he's down on earth leading the band...He's down there and she's up in spaceLet's go baby to that placeGarble the babble in the galactic theaterThe universe on center stageComing around to the end of the age - yea

HALL OF MIRRORS - EVERYONE IS DISTORTED -first in 2D in the mirror, then in 3D in the morph program Clanging bells and alarms, a deep drone.

The EXIT PORTALS dilate open.
CONSOLE: YOU MAY EXIT

ZOOM IN on one of the Viewscreens in a Superseat, see screen divide into
sections, each one a different character-figure.BILLI don't know. The money
-- its so much -
OSCARDOOR NUMBER ONE DOOR NUMBER TWO DOOR NUMBER THREE?The
Exterior doors open, leading back out to the corrimeter.
OSCARSurvey says: ALL THREE!USHERS appear at the doors, like sentries:

EST consists of 60 hours of intensive training, usually on two successive
weekends, where the initiate attempts to reach the goal of EST "getting it."
It is, however, never clear exactly what one gets, for Erhard's system is a
unique combination of Zen Buddhism, Scientology, and Vendanta Hinduism,
coupled with the power of positive thinking.
Erhard has said, "We want nothing short of a total transformation - an
alteration of substance, not a change of form" (Werner Erhard, What's So,
Jan. 1975). This alteration or transformation is accomplished during the
training sessions by attempting to change the individual's concept of who he
is. Once a person's belief system is shredded, the person becomes
vulnerable to accepting the ESTian world view.

What's at the end of this road? Your life!
The ride is what it's all about,
Looking back over the road to where you started.
From here to the end of the road is the best RIDE.
End to end a universe of MUDD
Its perimeter God its center: blood.

Visual: Spindly arms, bright light from behind
OSCAR
We will transform you in 60 hours - that's Summarian - so in summary you
aint seen nothing yet -- ARE YOU READY TO EVOLVE then COME ON~!

YOU WILL GET TO THE END OF YOUR LIVES - THE QUESTION IS - IN WHAT
CONDITION?The exit doors begin to open, letting light in.YOU ARE NOW
RELEASED TO GO BACK OUT INTO THE WORLD, BACK TO YOUR LIVESThe
doors open wider, admitting even more light. The AUDIENCE begins to rise,
moving toward the EXITS.The wind blows in.

THE SAUCER SPIN SLOWS DOWN AND the audience are seen, back in their
seats.

OSCARDOOR NUMBER ONE DOOR NUMBER TWO DOOR NUMBER THREE?The
Exterior doors open, leading back out to the corrimeter.
OSCARSurvey says: ALL THREE!USHERS appear at the doors, like sentries:

What's at the end of this road?
Your life!The ride is what it's all about,
Looking back over the road to where you started.
From here to the end of the road is the best RIDE.

End to end a universe of MUDD
Its perimeter God its center: blood.

Visual: Spindly arms, bright light from behind
OSCAR
YOU WILL GET TO THE END OF YOUR LIVES - THE QUESTION IS - IN WHAT
CONDITION?

The exit doors begin to open, letting light in.

YOU ARE NOW RELEASED TO GO BACK OUT INTO THE WORLD, BACK TO
YOUR LIVES

The doors open wider, admitting even more light. The AUDIENCE begins to
rise, moving toward the EXITS.The wind blows in.

BARRY
I just stopped by to see what condition my condition was in.

SHIELA
See you at the car.

You hacker you -

BARRY hacks into the central program of the saucer - millions of lines of
code -

The VIEWSCREENS are now open to the outside (or show an interior
projection of the exterior world, so that colors are computer enhanced and
give the day outside a super clarity)
Signs flash around the perimeter. English-style:

WAY OUT WAY OUT WAY OUT WAY OUT

Sub Message: WE CAN WORK TOGETHER TO WORK IT OUT AND MAKE IT
WORK!!!

BILLFar Out, far out.EXTERIOR. IN THE CORRIMETER. MARONG STEWART
STORE.AUDIENCE MEMBERS look at the new Estate II computers.

INT. THE SAUCER CORRIMETER.

BARRY sits down in one of the restaurant areas. He looks around, amazed at
the freshness of things, the newness.

FOSS
With your new vision, you will be looking for new work, yes?

BARRY

Yea, I was just thinking of that! Amazing!

FOSS
We want you to come work for us.

BARRY(interested, amused his way)As what?FOSSAs sales manager. We will give you the North American continent territory.FOSS hands him a Marong Stewart cardFOSSCall me. So we can work out the details.

Monty Hall (Monty Python) style
EXT. THE SAUCER MARKEE. NIGHT.The 360 display in markee motion shows the faces of all the audience members, scrolling by in the night.

OUTSIDE
TEDDYI'm running - for OFFICE!FOSSWhat's up?BARRYShe is. The sky. The Universe. My pecker. The electorate. They are waiting for the End of the Election, for the End of the World 0 digital at 11:00
THE CASH CODE is located in the Marong Stewart Central Program which is located INSIDE the SAUCER PROGRAM OF EVOLUTION

FOSS
We want you to help us set up a sales and installation network.

BARRY

YEA? What's your target market?

FOSS
The saucers, all their audiences - what they can compute together - now that's a MARKET! Influencing the whole planet -- the entire world!

FOSS types out a spate of information, displayed right-reading on BARRY'S screen RGB. BARRY types out the parameters of an eco market curve. FOSS looks and nods.

BARRY
OK, then. Super sales.

FOSS
What do you make of that?

BARRY
Everything -- if it's to work.

FOSSThe question is: do we believe it will work?

THE SEAL (OF THE SAUCER) sung by MARONG STEWART
My name is the Beast
I come from the EastI come with a planI got this planIt includes all of manIn it you reap what you sowThe music was funky, oh so New YorkyThey played it with a bump and a grindCome on First of MayGive me the World in my own

wayYou know, you know 'cause it's mineThe babies are waking, their phosphenes are wakingThey been dreaming of the Seal

LIGHT SHINES IN THROUGH THE EXIT PORTALS. The audiences rises to file out.

Now that you have learned play -- You should all be feeling better -than ever before in your life. Go out and get a good life.

We need the earth Mother, the GAIA, and the counterforce, and the Balance

COLLAPSING EST ONTO TRADITIONAL DRAMATIC STRUCTURE – THE MINI MOVIE SERIES
OSCAR
You all want to learn something about yourselves - about life -

This is THEATER - this is Interaction - THIS IS learning ABOUT EACH OTHER - each of us - we're all in the same - saucer -

SIGN: INTERMISSIONINT. THE CORRIMETER.

GO HAVE A GOOD BREAK - THEN CCOME BACK TO THE THEATER

BARRY walks up to ADELLE.
BARRY
Say, what do you think of the Show so far? Are you a character on the stage of life?

ADELLE
Very disturbing.ADELLE turns away.

BARRY
Hey, I didn't mean anything. I was just -- being friendly.

ADELLE
I know your kind of friend.

BARRY
Upset, I guess.

EXT. BOOM.

FOSS
We need all the good sales interface people. The ones on the markee. The ones in the Audience Zone.

MUNICIPAL BUILDING. A large sign is prominent: JOBS HEREA long line of job hopefuls. There is a department store window filled with TV's. The people in line watch the array of screens. The screens show the saucer SPOT

Nobody wants to BE the monster - begins to be "under the bell jar" suction - see themselves as beautiful - anorexic distortion - always see yourself as fat - mind mirror image - one of always being heavier than you are - solid bones without flesh - refuse to see what is true - create another identity - perhaps an alien - Don't cut me up

TEDDY

WE SHOULD BE HELPING EACH OTHER!

INT. THE SAUCER.

NIGHT.Around the contrayors and corrimeter, MUMBLING people, SHUFFLING around in a room, lack of ENERGY. The BEAM passes by outside, traveling horizontally.

INT. MARONG STEWART TRAINING -- "THE SALES BRIGADE"

DAY

AIDE
Selling the saucer?
Are you here for the MS Personaliy Test?

RODNEY
What does MS stand for? Multiple Sclerosis or something?

AIDE
Marong Stewart. A corporationm formed in 2010 in Delaware.

ALTON
Of the ware - I get it. The 'Stateware or whatever.

AIDE
Give me your names, please.

RODNEY
Rodney Barrett and Alton Shiner.

AIDE
Give me five. Dollars that is. Anew life for you now. Me - excel? That's aganst my hang-out religion.How many here want to SUCCEED.

One of the GIRLS blushes. Turns her head.A few hands raise.

CARL
bgggYea I--

AIDE
Do you want to --Do you want to succeed? Do you want to make a lot of
money?

ALTON
I'm sick of being paid shit wages

AIDE
Then you've come to the right place, don'tyou think?

ALTON
What do you pay?

AIDE
Fifty percent commission on order, and we get paid in cash at the end of the
first week.

RODNEY
Jeez, can't beat that

AIDE
Get you badges.
RODNEYWhat do we do?
AIDE has two ID cards prepared for them, instant cardS to wear on their
shirts.
BIOFEEDBACK MONITORS are attached to their heads (which are actually
EEG scanners)
Then BARRY enters and walks to the front of the room.
OSCAR appears behind him.
All hand raise
BARRYHow many people do we have here who want toSUCCEED?

BARRYHow many are ready to fight and die to succeed?No hands raise.

BARRY
That's the difference between those who just think they want to succeed and
those who really mean it. By the end of the training, you'll all raise your
hands on the second question.Now what do you think of that information?

RODNEYI love to be in formation with my favoritegirl.BARRYInformation is
POWER. Repeat after me:

ALL INFORMATION IS POWER.

RECRUITSINFORMATION IS POWER!

INFORMATIONIS POWER INFORMATION IS POWER.RODNEYI still want to be
in formation with my favorite girl.

"SAUCER SEASON" There is a time for Saucer SeasonThere is a time for saucer seasonTo every saucer there is a reasonWill you be there for the maiden voyage?

EXTERIOR, DAY. OUTSIDE THE SAUCER.MEDIA POV:SWEEP OF COVERAGE OVER THE CROWD SPEWING FROM THE SAUCER DOORS.The first of the 7,992 AUDIENCE MEMBERS begin emerging into the strong sunlight of mid-day, looking around, blinking.

BILL runs along, waving his arms, toward the parked cars.BILLHey, I feel renewed!MARTHA runs after him.

MARTHA
Yes, I feel refreshed - ready to takeon anything.

SHIELA
Was it worth $500?

The AUDIENCE members are all grinning. Running, cavorting.They begin singing the round "Row row your boat" then begin substituting "saucer" for "boat."

THE SALES MARKS line up to buy the ESTATE II accessories, using their MARONG STEWART debit cards to purchase.

INT. THE SAUCER.

Background, alien workers hose down the stage from the mock carnage of the last of the acts before

Projection #1.TEDDY

                              What do we do now?OSCARWe call it creating the reality you choose to live in.

TEDDY
You're not going to take over the world in front of my face.

OSCAR
We might - I'm not. Hold space for a minute. I'll be right back

EXT. THE PARKING LOT.

SHIELA and BARRY in the car.BARRYGotta go get the kids.SHIELAI CAN'T WAIT - TO TELL THEM.BARRYWhat?SHIELAEverything.BARRYI can't wait -- to get a new job.SHIELAYOU WILL?BARRYWill I ever.INTERIOR. BILL and MARTHA.MARTHAWant to feel my software?BILLYou want support from the hardware.INTERMISSIONAUDIENCE members run to phones (LONG LINES) to make calls to relative, baby sitters, etc.CLOSE ON DAK WILLARD on

phone.CELL MAGNET: (SPEAKS, A RESONANT DRONE))The Crystal Amulet Will Show The RayEDITOR (V0)What's it like?
DAK
A cross between Living Theater, Broadway musical and confrontational whatever -- reality TV from last decade.

EDITORLike life, so stay there and live it. I'll give you front page sidebars.

EXT. DAY. THE GLADE.OSCAR and TEDDYOSCARWhat are you geunning away from.TEDDYFrom you - from this whole big ship thing - from my wife's hallucinations -Getting back to the real world.OSCARAre you sure that's where you want to be?TEDDYThat's where I AM - I have been held back too long - I deserve to work with the -PEOPLE.WOMANIt's going on - how long? I don't know.INT. SAUCER. NIGHT.OSCAR and ELDERS, above the saucer arena.ELDERWe need a kicker.OSCARWhat?ELDERSSomething to get it moving.OSCARTheir culture seems to be based on extreme opposites. How about the Beast-Savior combo.ELDERThen we might need an "earth mother" - if you know what I mean.OSCARI see - "Mars Needs Women" - huh?ELDERThey seem obsessed, according to the lit, of invaders getting into their biopak's pants.OSCARA little shape changing, morphing - substitute - that what you mean.ELDEREven though it's not you, the woman must THINK that she wants you - so she will be THINKING of you while her mate - ah - OSCARSo we can glimpse our genetic code on the offspring, eh?ELDERPrecisely. Exactly.

LINES OF CODE, STRETCHING AROUND THE BLOCK, THE TEATER MARKEE OF THE SAUCERTHE SALES MARKS line up to buy the ESTATE II accessories, using their MARONG STEWART debit cards to purchase.

POWER bible

INT. NIGHT. THE STAGE ARENA.Alien GROUNDIES hose down the central stage from the mock carnage of the preceding acts.OSCAR sees GWEN wandering around the stage area. The ALIEN GROUNDIES are hosing down the stage from the mock carnage of the preceding acts.OSCAR (TO HIMSELF)There's the Earth Mother.He walks in a wide arc, gradually moving in toward her. She notices that he is approaching when he is only a few yards away.GWENOh!OSCAR smiles a big-grin-warm smile. Relaxing. Inviting.GWEN sees OSCAR and gets up, walking over to him.GWEN stops, OSCAR turns and notices her.OSCARGwen -- right?GWENHow did you know?OSCAR(points to his head) Audience list - (pause)You are lovely -- for an earth woman.GWENThank you. (pause) Do you aliens have wives?OSCARJust one. Separated.GWENYou have children?OSCARYes. I never see them. In another galaxy, far away.GWENYou miss them?OSCAROf course. And you?GWENNot yet. I lost a baby.OSCARYour husband did not appreciate that. That is why you are here?GWENPart of it. Relationships just seem to - wear out - after time.OSCARIt is difficult. Your culture is based on money, and you don't - contribute?GWENWell -- that's Teddy. Worried about everything -- especially the bills.You're very charismatic.OSCAR (BOWING SLIGHTLY)Thanks you. You are very beautiful - for an earth woman.

GWENThanks. My husband doesn't appreciate my - beauty.OSCARThat may be. But YOU are the aliens here, and we love you.Do you get it?GWENI don't know what I get. Not much from Teddy.OSCARNothing more alien than a couple of estranged humans.GWENYes to "work it out." Or just avoid the whole problem.OSCARWe cannot consort with the audience members. It is against our First Directive.GWENSo - it's just all theater.OSCARThat - and perhaps more.Be your own children. Listen to them. They will tell you when the Show is about to begin.GWEN and the ALIEN OSCAR together, looking at each other.OSCAR teaches GWEN to BLINK.OSCARThis is how we communicate with the eyes.GWEN (BLINKING)Nobody loves no-one.

GWEN
Are you the savior or the devil?

OSCA
Are you sure there is either?

OSCAR
If I were your husband, I would appreciate you.

GWEN
I'm not always the easiest to get along with.

OSCAR

I can take you higher. Love lifts us up where it belong.

GWENSounds like a song, yes? (amused)You do bring a smile to my face.

OSCARLike a candy?He takes a spirulina-like saucer-shaped lozenges from his pouch.GWENIt is all right for humans?OSCAROf course - nothing better. We're all - carbon based - humanoid. There are other life bases, yet in this csae, the two populations are at least that similar.GWEN(takes the candy)OSCARDo you smoke?

GWENQuitting. Constantly quitting.OSCAR takes two Bidi-like green cigarettes from his other pouch.OSCARJoin me?GWENThis isn't that dope stuff is it?OSCAR(shakes his head)No just herbs from our home planet. Very healthy for all living creatures.OSCAR gives her the weed-smoke. He brings forth a smooth lighter, which ignites with two flames, drugstore-soda like, and he lights her cigarette and his at the same time, looking deep into her eyes.GWEN blushes, coughing.GWENWhat is this?OSCARYou're get to like it. It helps to raise consciousness. It's like brain money.

GWENI could sure use some if that.

OSCAR offers her his arm. They walk across the STAGE.

OSCAR
Oh - and I can teach you to blink. Think and blink.GWENWhat's that?OSCARA way to reconstruct yourself. Think it and blink it. It manifests.GWENLike a manifesto?OSCARA little more. Reinvention, regeneration, re-creation.GWEN puts her hand on his arm, feeling the flesh slightly.GWENYou don't feel too alien.Maybe you can help me find my husband.He left in the middle of one of those Acts.OSCARCaught up in the Acts - they are for communication.GWENYea, but we don't really communicate.OSCARLike two different cultures. Nothing more estranged than a couple of alien humans.GWENHe can't make the connection.OSCARYou're better because you can't have him -- or his children?That does not make sense.GWENRightOSCARThen become your own children.Become children again.Give birth to yourselves.
INT. NIGHT -

GWENYou're not serious.OSCARI am seriously serious.GWENI think you are. Oh I feel so woozy - so free!She faints into his arms. OSCAR continues walking with GWEN draped over his arm.OSCARLearn to think, learn to blink.
I am Sirius.
You are your own children here. Your children will show you the way, with child-like wonder.
INT. FANTASY SPACEL
OVER'S TRYST - LEAP

INT. DAY. A WHITE CUBICAL-CORRIDOR.

MARONG STEWART TRAINING.
An antiseptic hospital-like "training" environment, no windows, artificial light.

TRAINER
OK, now I'm not here for a long time, I'm here for a GOOD time!(cheers hoops & hollers)

Welcome to INFO CENTER MARKETING, brought to you by Marong Stewart. I'm into girls and Messaging Interface 0 how about you?

The Song of Self is
MI-MI-MI-MI-MI-MI - "I'm into MI(me)"Whoo - I just got back from Arabia, from a big arms deal, and are my arms TIRED. So I'm your super salesman - I can sell icecubes to an Eskimo, a glass of water to a drowning man...We need to get you aligned, lined up like a team

RODNEY
There is no "I" in fuck you - AND your TEAM

RODNEY
There is no I in fuck you too

BARRY
You will learn to create from nothing
Just as God did

ALTON
There was something there. God just shaped it?

ESTATE II spots projected silently on sidewalls show their media clout.I feel
so SAD for you - I have SO MUCH going on
Inside my head - and you just have the money, the
Deals and the culture of BUSINESS - self-centered worth
Which is WORT-less.

Want something better? Follow the bouncing ball - the planet earth
GAIA is PISSED OFF
She will shake you like a wild bronco throws a cowboy
And STOMP on you, whoop your ASS!

BARRY
My lovely wife Shiela will coordinate the computer setup for the entire
extruded supra organization.

So you will know how to follow through as multi-level...
Marketing

MANAGERS
Say that in fucking English or Tagalo, please, for our customer service
outsources tucan understand. Share the joke with the class, amateurs.

ALTON
In fo' what?

RODNEY
I like to be "in formation" with my girl friend.

BARRY
That is so fucking OLD. Some of you will be chosen to join The Brigade, our
hand-selected premier marketing outfit. We have picket them to do the
marketing security operations, much as the Rolling Stones hired the Hell's
Angels to police Altamont - back in the antiquity of mass events

FOSS
That's what we've been told - excuse me while I collect my consultant check

BARRY
Did you have BILLING on your mind?

INT. TRAINING AREA.
(LATER)They find RODNEY and ALTON's video helmets.SLUG #1Hey what's
this?SLUG #2Do you know what we got here?INFORM-ers.ALTON

I always like to be IN FORM with my best girl, sometimes TWOGROUP laughs.SLUG #2That's getting old.SAXTake 'em to the boiler room.

1. Humanity and Planet Earth are currently going through a huge change or shift in consciousness and reality perception.
2. The Mayan civilization of Central America was and is the most advanced in relation to time-science knowledge. Their main calendar is the most accurate on the planet. It has never erred. They actually have 22 calendars in total, covering the many timing cycles in the Universe and Solar System. Some of these calendars are yet to be revealed.
3. The Mayan fifth world finished in 1987. The sixth world starts in 2012. So we are currently "between worlds". This time is called the "Apocalypse" or revealing. This means the real truth will be revealed. It is also the time for us to work through "our stuff" individually and collectively.
4. The Mayan sixth world is actually blank. This means it is up to us, as co-creators, to start creating the new world and civilization we want now.
5. The Mayans also say that by 2012-
- we will have gone beyond technology as we know it.
- we will have gone beyond time and money.
- we will have entered the fifth dimension after passing through the fourth dimension
- Planet Earth and the Solar System will come into galactic synchronization with the rest of the Universe.
- Our DNA will be "upgraded" (or reprogrammed) from the centre of our galaxy. (Hunab Ku)
"Everbody on this planet is mutating. Some are more conscious of it than others. But everyone is doing it" - Extraterrestrial Earth Mission.
6. In 2012 the plane of our Solar System will line up exactly with the plane of our Galaxy, the Milky Way. This cycle has taken 26,000 years to complete. Virgil Armstrong also says that two other galaxies will line up with ours at the same time. A cosmic event!
7. Time is actually speeding up (or collapsing). For thousands of years the Schumann Resonance or pulse (heartbeat) of Earth has been 7.83 cycles per second, The military have used this as a very reliable reference. However, since 1980 this resonance has been slowly rising. It is now over 12 cycles per second! This mean there is the equalivant of less than 16 hours per day instead of the old 24 hours.
8. During the Apocalypse or the time "between worlds" many people will be going through many personal changes. The changes will be many and varied. It is all part of what we came here to learn or experience. Examples of change could be- relationships coming to an end, change of residence or location, change of job or work, shift in attitude or thinking etc.
9. Remember, in any given moment we are making small and large decisions. Each decision is based on LOVE or FEAR. Choose love, follow your intuition, not intellect and follow your passion or "burning inner desire." Go with the flow.
10. Thought forms are very important and affect our everyday life. We create our reality with thought forms. If we think negative thoughts of others this is what we attract. If we think positive thoughts we will attract positive people and events. So be aware of your thoughts and eliminate the unnecessary negative or judgemental ones.

11. Be aware that most of the media is controlled by just a few. Use discernment! Look for the hidden agendas. Why is this information being presented to you? What is "their" real agenda? Is it a case of problem-reactionsolution? Do "they" create a problem so that "we" react and ask for a fix, then "they" offer their solution? The "solution is what "they" really wanted in the first place.
12. Remember almost nothing happens by accident. Almost all "events" are planned by some agency or other. Despite this, it is a very exciting time to be alive!

EXT. DAY. A WAREHOUSE COMPLEX. BRIGADE TRAINING HQ.Pounding "Windows 95-98" music, the Frankie Lane, "Rawhide" mixed with Peter Gunn soundtrack

Musical cue - this should get a laugh from the audience, mixed with the image of Power Steeds saddled and ridden by blue-armored "salesmen" with side carts carrying the "heads" of Estate II organic microcomputers.

NOTE: The Brigade sequences should be filmed in a monochrome filtered way, like a dark sepia or some other color (i.e a better version-form of the trick used in Angry Red Planet)

OSCAR$
It's all magic. You have to be there when it happens to see the Magic.

POWERSTEEDS

A convoy of POWER STEEDS, half horse, half truck, armadillo-like scale-covered bodies, a large truck like extension on the end, pod-saddles above, one KNIGHT-LIKE Brigade member, Samurai-looking, atop the highest saddle, the smaller GREYS in the PODS on the Power Steed, ready to roll over the countryside and bring humanity to its knees.SOUND: "WINDOWS" soundtrack beat.EGO and SAX front the BRIGADE sitting around, drinking beer, looking at a wooden-wire frame model of the SAUCER which looks like it was built by aborigines, tying the sticks and wood together, a "wooded wireframe" emulation of the saucer configuration.

EXT. SUBURBAN "PRINTED CIRCUIT" NEIGHBORHOOD. EVENING.CARS are pulling into driveways: it is supper time. SAX and EGO lead the marketing team. FARO's face in a porta-computer monitor, mouths advice, which SAX monitors in his headphones.SAXAll right, OK, feel uptight in every way.THE BRIGADE stands ready. EGO lobs a mortar shell toward the front door, which bursts, opening the door.

The BRIGADE rushes the property. HUSBAND, WIFE and CHILD look out the front door. See the rush of BRIGADE coming.

SAX

Where is the nearest electrical outlet. The den? The Living room?
The FAMILY cower.
The BRIGADE members scatter into the other rooms.
BRIGADE MEMBERHere it is!EGO slams an INSTALLER into the wall, putting a huge power source where they're had been a small outlet. He plugs the ESTATE II computer into it.The FAMILY are rounded up and shoved together into the room with EGO.

EGO (A MOCKERY OF AD COPY, THROUGH CLENCHED TEETH)
This is the Estate II organic micro computer. It can compute at speeds equal to or even surpassing that of the human brain. We suggest you take your payment coupons and use your computer. Do not miss a payment.

The FAMILY cowers in a corner as the BRIGADE do their work. Cable is unrolled. The satellite monitors of the main Estate II are placed in each room of the house.

EGO
Now you have full coverage.

EXT(s). DAY. "INTERMISSION" VARIOUS LOCATIONS.LONG LANDSCAPES - Midwest, East Coast, Southwest. Stragglers, bedraggled, worn-torn, hitchhiking down the wide expanses of NEWROUTESSIGNS: "ANYWHERE BUT HERE"

ADELLE "HUIT" EIGHT-8

Like LADY GAGA -aggressive, female performer - from shy wallflower

ADELLE
Tinkle those 88's mothafucka -

ADELLE "Graps" GOD-FUK The Video

PULL BACK TO SHOW ENTIRE GLORIOUS COSMOS GLEAMING

OSCAR
What a conclusion to reach - so says the alien-fight regressive evolution with a checkup and a check - we're only here for the money

MINI-MOVIE 4 THE ALIEN HEIST

GRAY RETICULI
The Gay K K is our kind of group- both liberal and corrupt

GRAY R2
Jip Jump Jive don't Care If I Die

GRAY RETICULI

We can rip this planet off and they won't even know it

MARONG STEWART
Defenses are down - let's go to town

Our CURRENCY is LEAVES

GR2
LEAVES of GRASS

MS
If they only knew - if money grew on trees - and it DOES - there's be more
of them. And this planet would treat them better.
They go around the saucer - the Superseats are the way we can plant
subliminal, behavioral cues - they will follow then outside the SHOW into
their personal LIVES

INT. SAUCER

OSCAR
MOCALOHA, Ma.n Do you best then do your do. Do your done. I believe in
every-One!

TEDDY
Crash and burn.

OSCAR
That's as in crash AND burn.

EXT. CITY STREET. NIGHT

The window filled with banks of TV's all showing an ad: KAKA BANK Line of
Credit

LINE UP AND SIGN UP : THE PITCH

CRAZY MAN'S WAY TO RICHES - MAKE 1,000 A DAY - CALL 1-999-123-
4567THE MONEY SYSTEM TAPES $39.95 - GET YOURS NOW!

INT. DAY. THE BRIGADE CAMP HQ.

SA(a checklist)
Authomatic dialers, groupmind customer service,

WOODEN "WIREFRAME" OF SAUCER 1/2 SCALE MOCKUP -The Brigade is
engaged in attacking this fake saucer as an exercise for their eventual
assault.

SAX and EGO are seen close, in non-specific setting at first. Dark, silhouetted, inscrutable as cockroaches, Palmetto bugs, ready to fly.They have electric LED eyes, various colors, blue and red, some green, varying degrees of status shown by the eyes.

PULL BACK during their cut shows the cavernous SAN LUIS OBISPO WAREHOUSE with a huge Macy's-like rubber figure floating in the background.

For any eventuality.

This is closed source code, so if you don't make your payments you will be thrown off the InfoNet. You would not want that to happen.

PAY UP or check out.

INT. DAY/NIGHT. THE BOILER ROOM SATELLITE.

RODNEY and ALTON are hustled into the airlock waiting area from the SHUTTLE which is visible outside. We turn around as they are manhandled around to SEE what they SEEAn up-sloping floor which has smoked glass, the outer rim of a large circular SPACE STATION. There is a ROW of DESKS on either side of the central aisle. An orange carpet on the "floor."
They are PUSHED up the aisle to where a hunched, cigarette-smoking woman is leaning over one of the CALLER's desks, listening in on a separate phone headpiece.

She TURNS to see RODNEY and ALTON being pushed along by the BRIGADE member.

RODNEY
Hi.

ALTON
Oh! Witch's brew. "I'm melting I'm melting."

DESTY looks at them.BRIGADE MEMBERInfiltrators. Put them to work. They are indentured for training foe the training.DESTYOK - ah some young, pretty ones. Well, my pretties, I'll GET YOU.DESTYPart one of your training. Stay put and WATCH ME.DESTY walks the revolving space-station phone room, looking at the cluttered desks on either side. (A semi-quote of the "jogging" sequence from 2001)PHONE CALLERS hunched at desks call down through a list of computer-generated names.PITCHER (BRITISH VOICE)Hello, is the lady of the house at 'ome?WOMANYes.PITCHERWe're having a special sale this week only - you can get an Estate II organic microcomputer with full organic software package for only $6,667.77 cent - how's that sound?WONANI'd have to ask my husband.The SPEAKER PHONE lets them all, including us, listen. RODNEY and ALTON mock interest, leaning forward to listen.DESTY (GRABBING THE PHONE)Is that MIKE, your SECOND HUSBAND who does not know that his "son" is really the bastard left over from that FIRST marriage to the drug-dealer named Tom who never came home and eventually left you and the baby, who thinks the child is his

because you never TOLD HIM?WOMANI - I - how much do I pay.DESTYYou will receive your payment coupon book - it has all 900 payment slips neatly arranged by due date. Just send in the payments on time and we WON'T have to release any information to your husband-slop Tom to blow your cover and upset the apple cart, OK?WOMAN (ON THE VIDEO SPEAKERPHONE SCREEN, ANGUISHED FACE, TEARS WELLING UP))OKDESTYSLAM MARKETING - Yea!ALTONWow - sex SELLS!
OSCAR (ON VIDEO SCREEN, LIKE STEVE JOBS)We are bringing a new prosperity and ABUNDANCE to your planetWe are making it all AROUND you - on earth and in the sky

At the end you will all be named STEVE and you will all have JOBS!

EXT. DAY. EARTH - THE GROVE

.

OSCAR
You are the cherub, hiding out in the woods.
(holds up Bicycle card)
Here's your bicycle - turn it sideways, and it is the profile of the flying saucer theater.

TEDDY
I am running for President on the Old Love, New Peace Initiative - to end the warring - forever.

OSCARYou must wake up and WIN.
You must be in tune with Universal Law.

TEDDYPaint it black, you Devil.

OSCARNo YOU paint it black.

TEDDY looks. The walls of the bar become black. Dayglo psychedelic posters appear and roll down the walls.

INT. "DAY" - THE SAUCER THEATER.

OSCARIn my most indwelling spirit, across the universe, I hold you to your promise to Complete the Show.TEDDYI never made any promise.OSCARYou bought the ticket.

KAKA BANK - the system melts down - cities shimmer as in heat rising, like mind desert - there are CARD READERS on the bank teller machines - diffraction codes worn on the foreheads of the despositors -In the middle of the scene - like OZ - a hotair balloon sits on a platform, ready to launch - Daddy Warbucks (OSCAR) wearing large dollar-sign glasses - hands ADELLE the Key to the City
OSCARHere you take this - it won't be worth much now

BARRYYea, back to the original $24 paid for by the Dutch to get this island of granite and ego -

ADELLE with a Number One hit is on stage with her headset and outfit on – now taking the little dance she did in the Saucer up to an entire new level –

OSCAR/GWEN in CYBER SUMIT SPACEOSCARCan you get him back? I can't.GWENWish I could.I can't make Teddy do anything. That's up to you.OSCARMaybe we can - I, we, need him. There is a numerology to the show, with the Lottery, and everything - transformation comes with a very balanced spin - the difference of even one could make all the difference in the - world. The universe, the outcome. Oh well, time to create from nothing.
GWENWhat? Where are you going?OSCARTo create a ruse. Excuse me - when the teacher is ready, the student appears.
GWEN
Everything is a circle – everything moves in cycles -

EXT. DAY. THE FOREST GLADE.
Alien machinery, a large weird looking SKIDDER. Trees covered with translucent bags.

TEDDY checks it out. WATCHES as the aliens strip a grove of green trees of their chlorophyl, leaving them blanched.See through

OSCAR
We use the fractal trees in the moiré zone to grow the organic microprocessors that drive the Estate II AND the contrabators of the superstarship. Money is leaves, leaves of green, I know you're there. This is for YOU

TEDDY
The Estate II's are taking over the economy - the global economy -

OSCAR
The Globe. The Globe is Theater. Globe Theater. Live Earth Drama.
This is OUR form of money.
The saucer has been dark for the Summer. Now it is going back into The Show again. The people are returning.

The alien sat on the open doorway to the corrimeter-saucer.

INT. THE SAUCER. "NIGHT"

LIGHTS FLASH THREE TIMES THREE TIMES IN SUCCESSION, NINE IN ALL: END OF INTERMISSION.The AUDIENCE are guided back to their seats by the USHERS with gestures & laser-pointers.OSCAR expands out into twelve clones of himself. Orange, like Hari Krsna's

OSCAR
we all have a Saucer Name - punch your names into the keyboards at your seats.

CONSOLE READOUT:THE GANG'S ALL HEREHERE COMES EVERYBODYTO ALL WHO ARE ABOUT TO EVOLVECENTRAL CONSOLE READOUT:1:144FILL and HASS cross the stage in a fishing dinghy, with net, casting the waters.FILLFisher of men's souls.HASSTake the seven we caught - go feed the multitude.

Seven times seven times seven. Exponential growth to a point beyond the future.

FILL
It's not feeding time at the zoo - yet.

HASS
Animal husbandry.

The ALIEN STOOGES come in from the sidelines.

STOOGESSold to the man in the spittoon haircut.

FILL
The Eraserhead of Wipout –

OSCAR surfing on the crest of the MEDIA wave –

OSCAR
I am ahead of the curve! What is your estimated time of evolvel?

CARL
Yo, so there how you DOIN, man? I seen you before haven't I? You have? My name is Son of Earth. Better than Son of Sam, he be a murderer crazy—I got the women, one black and one Spanish—about this high—who loves to freak...Do the wild thing?Dat's it, the wild thing. They got pornos and some beer in the fridge—they like the cocaine, they put it on your power tower and lick it off while they go crazy—I never heard of any women like that—I got nothing but bitches and witches in my life—It's Gaia—she rub you down with petroleum and give you her hot gasses and even explode orgasmically right before your mother-fuckin eyes... we have old Cosmos tapes that she like to watch—gets off on Carl Sagan—I already donated to the alienating society—I gave them my watch and my reviewer, Dak Willard—he's theirs now... That's one less reviewer and more shows that can go on cause a bad review can kill a show just like you'd like to kill your Earth—It doesn't sound like any planet I ever knew or heard of—It's your Mother, man, and she be wanting it—rape

me again, she's cryin—it'll only take ten billion to make it right—you give me the ten—we'll all take turns—I'll get the stuff from my Man down the street—I'll be back here in ten minutes or ten million years—drive that pussy—drive that pussy—cause pussy don't know what it wants, not even Mother Gaia—and three pussy the trinity don;t know more than two pussy what it want—it know less than anything—Procreative potential packs a punch—Sex sells, man—experience man—that's what does it—She got the Experience—she can freak every day and still bounce back for more—-jus' give her a rest once an awhile, tha's all, like letting the worn-out soil replenish itself—she freak every day—streets and highways—clogged with bottlenecked traffic—gas guzzling road warriors—on the unlimited speed SKYWAY-—I got the blues, the saucer blues, Man, so when you COMING DOWN? I got cramps and I about to kill somebody—so get down here now—Oh, no, Men be ready—waiting for us now—we're wasting time—Men and the girls—so come on, man, let's have the green so we can get the Right Stuff-—we can get really FUCKED UP on the saucer stuff-—on every street corner you can find a little green man selling it—-for the Gaia punch, man, so she can take out drills and our shafts over and over again—what is the Planet Man's burden? To get off this silly rock before we wreck and ruin our own chances for survival. But there are catches, yes there are. Yes, like the Doomsday Asteroid, you'll be right back, huh, coming right up—yea—I know all about it—I heard every line—I seen every headline—it's the bad news squelches the Good News—It's Gaia Paranoia—Like the moth to the flame, man, like the moth to the flame—so the saucer rap is on—like how's your fine SELF tonight, baby—where you gain now and will you know who you are when you get there? You read philosophy books, man? Well, I got a whole book in my head you ought to read. It's philosophy of the streets, man. Like, I was a pimp and a dealer. Dealt gray-market drugs and European import cars. Man, we could do good in a good week. A few thousand dol-

SHIELA

INT. THE SAUCER STAGE. NIGHT.

FOUNTAINS RISE (as in Disneyland) as OSCAR and GWEN dance through the spotlights like Ginger Rogers and Fred Astaire. The FOUNTAINS dispense champaigne.

A LARGE WEDDING CAKE platform rising, circled in lights, stocking-clad alien DANCERS, Rockettes-style, lifting and kicking legs in time with the music. BIG BAND sound.CARMEN MIRANDA-like alien with exotic off-world fruit on her large HAT in a BUSBY BERKELEY-like musical number.

I am money I don't want to stop the show
I am money or your life, don't you know...

TEDDY
I'M NOT BIG INTO GOD

OSCAR
That's why we call it the Saucer Season -

I want to start the BLISS - I got the Bliss so much I don't know what to -

Song: SAUCER ROULETTE

ADELLE
I'm afraid.OSCARI think depressed maybe.Just like your life on the road is an adventure, you can have adventure WITHIN your life, every day. Challenge, reprisals, whatever turns you on.

ADELLE
Follow the yellow brick road?

OSCAR
What's that?

ADELLE
My favorite film when I was a little girl. Somewhere over the rainbow.

OSCAR
Oh the ruby slippers. OK – I remember once `
(they appear on her feet)
Click them together

ADELLE clicks

OSCAR
There's no place like home

ADELLE
There's no place like home.

OSCAR
And home is the entire Universe!

The audience FILES TOWARD THE EXITS.

Sound of talking, murmur of post-Show conversation.The EXITS open. The moving aisle deliver people up to the corrimeter.OSCAR, on stage, watches.DAK WILLARD Heads to the men's room. There is a line in front of OUT OF ORDER signs. He is still tipsy.An USHER approaches DAKDAKWhat is that pattern on the ceiling - the dome - of the saucer?USHERThe Seal of the Saucer, a light-illuminated mandala similar to a...DAKI need to use the restroom.USHERPlumbing's backed up.You wouldn't want to go in there.DAKThis is super technology -- you don't get problems like this. You must have other facilities.USHERAll closed.DAKIt can't be! I just gulped a beer at that rip-off counter, and I need to take a leak!USHERYou'll have to wait. Return to your seat. The Show is about to start again.

DAK

What are you talking about! This is high technology. You don't have
problems like that.

CENTRAL CONSOLE READOUT - PRESENTATION: THE UNIVERSE

OSCAR

(laser light pointer)

Now for the next step the near group of galaxies. The cluster of galaxies
appears in the center of the saucer stage arena.

The audience is jolted to awareness by the CELL MAGNET passing over them,
an eerie yellow beam emanating from it.

OSCAR
We are a spiritual brotherhood - a collection of benevolent planets - the
Ashtar Command is here to help you through the final portal into the new
universe - in total transition

BARRY
It's the 1111, the 11:11 That's the program of the saucer – it's a Parity
Problem – it's the lack of communication between two parts -

TEDDY
BIPOLAR ALIENS - Good vs. Evil - within themselves - they represent the
entire moral order - you think it makes a difference? You think you can
prepare yourself to enter eternity, or the universe?

OSCAR
Theater - the final frontier -

COUNTDOWN CLOCK: 52.45.20 AND COUNTING

INT. THE SAUCER -- 'NIGHT'
The CELL MAGNET revolves on its boom glowing down on theparticipants,
bathing them in an eerie red light.

OSCAR
Now -- you can free yourselves --forever -- by releasing your own energies -
- or remain eternally blocked -- merging all the indigo and crystal energies,
the get ready for the Great Ascension

NO SOUND: Hushed silence

OSCAR
We can start now or end forever our going!

CELL MAGNET zooms in on MARTHA and BILL.MARTHA

Get an airline ticket and fly away -

FOSS and the BRIGADE walk down the aisles with BULLHORNS telling everyone to empty their pockets

INT. "DAY" - THE SAUCER THEATER. CELL MAGNET BEAM on CARL.

CARL
I'm sorry about the talk the other night --our vibes were less than perfect.

OSCARWhat are you going to DO about it?OSCARI didn't Mean to make you cry - Didn't mean to make you --feel that way.CARLWhat about the breakdowns?OSCARYou mean --about your needs?

CARL
No -- my plans.OSCARYou'll have to update them as necessary. There are no guarantees.CARLOnly that -- the show must go on?OSCARNot even that. CARL. Spill it.CARLSpill what, milk, blood?OSCARWhatever you choose.CARLI could have had a great weekend in Vegas for what this ersatz showcost..OSCARTHEN GO. You're in the know.I make no promises, no refunds.We have a saying on Vega . Looselytranslated: "Go with need." Go to Vegas

Close on CARL, CELL MAGNET POV.

CARL's RAP TO THE UNIVERSE
CARL
PAROUSIA: The event horizon, where material and spiritualplanes met -- the material/spiritual "sky"=9
OMEGA POINT-

Its such a carnival thing - all the people moving across the surface of the planet
                              Acting Out the realities

LIGHTS DIM. OVERHEAD SCROLLWORK BECOMES A HUGE CLOCK - SOUNDING OF ALARM CLOCK LIKE BIG BEN.

GWEN
(in center stage
I'm an ALIEN woman. I am the alien's WOMAN. Why won't you release me?

The Great Interface

The two-backed beast 3750

Universe from which all things come, right? Even men come from heaven, right? Sweet little girls, bundles of kisses and knows.

THUNDER and LIGHTNING

TEDDYWe are part of that universe, are you?GWENThat is not the purpose of the universeGonna blink it away - back to you, girlfriends.No lips no ears no eyes no face. as frightening as the end of the world is going to be --(she blinks her eyes at him)I am in charge of the whole. I am God. Open the door and in I come IN

GWEN
Nothing like the End of the World. Just do what I say. You might be BE OK. All sweetness and light. We must manifest.

EXT. NIGHT. UNDER THE STREET LAMPS.

MONEY rains out of the open sky. TEDDY stands there, basking in the green rays.

OSCAR's VOICE
It is the Money System!

TEDDY
I am going beyond the beyond!

GWENYou aren't going anywhere.

TEDDYDid you talk to me through the SKY? Did you communicate through the SUN?

DISSOLVE TO (ext radial park) CROWD REACTION.
Then we will have an end to nuclear arms buildup. Isn't it foolish, this distrust, this arming against potential? Nothing will ever come from using a nuclear missile. Let's agree to disagree, if necessary, and stop making them. Let's put the money and effort into human rights and human potential. The stars are much bigger than our territorial egos. We can share. During and after wars we are forced to share anyway. Let's start now.CROWD cheers.There really is such a thing; such a concept as "too late" and no one wants to live it. There is simply too much potential suffering to continue our fascination with "progress" through the nuclear and missile technologies. There are peaceful uses for our enthusiasms.We can still be provocative with each other, but we do not need to and should not want to risk the world for our goals.Because our goals are with the world and with the people.

APPLAUSE

TEDDY
We will wipe them out.

To the CENTER of the GALAXY?LIGHTNING and THUNDERTEDDYWhat world do we know that this could be the ending of? The beginning of what?GWENThe beginning of the end of time.TEDDYGWENTaking my face and giving it to an old hag. I don't want 50,000 wrinkles on my face.You have taken our love and ruined me.TEDDYI don't know these people you are ranting about.GWENThis will be my chosen state.Sharon and Nancy and all those others you took to avoid me.I will end the world, except for me and my son.EXT. DAYTEDDY sets up a "revival tent" outside of PEORIA, in a country pasture.CELL MAGNET outline hazy in the sky. They are on world "stage" -BANNERWE CAN WORK TOGETHER TO WORK IT OUT AND MAKE IT WORK.TEDDYI "got" it.OSCARGot what?TEDDYI got the Show the purpose the whatever. Move forward, make a difference, chose what IS and go work in IT. That's IT.OSCARWhat are you up to now?TEDDYThis is the "world level" now. This is playing a really "big game."OSCARThis is bullshit.TEDDYNot from what you've said, from what you're brought me to believe.OSCARI do not traffic in belief. I'm better at losing things. Like entire populations. Like the earth --TEDDYWe are green - we are all "babes in the woods" - that's my EXPERIENCE.OSCARYou only saw the show in avatar mode - simulacrum. That's like being hanged in effigy.You may overview the points but you rob yourself of the experience.TEDDYI am going for THE ONE.I will unite this planet into abundance - and do a dance - yea! A-BUN-DANCE. (shaking his hips, patting his butt) I GOT it.OSCARYou need to get a gripTEDDYWhatever that means. You see you want us all to "get" you but a lot of you is un-gettable.OSCARSounds like a personal problem to me.TEDDYI am "choosing what is" - I am getting away from a bad, dull marriage - I am choosing someone new - have you met Adelle.OSCARI know her from the saucer. You know that. We have the bio-readouts of all the participants who made it thought the lottery - we even have yours. It's ready for you - when you come back.TEDDYBut the saucer show is over - they got out. Adelle is my - CAMPAIGN manager - she is managing ME. I am going to run.OSCARFor?ADELLEI will run with you.OSCARTo or from - what?Is the Show ever really over? We'll see how much you carry away from it with you.It brings you to it, the Show is an Exchange.TEDDYYea?We have a spiritual war going on in the land. We need new blood. I am working to get people together to work it out and make it work.OSCARMake a difference?TEDDYSomething like that. Yea.OSCARThat's old language, something from our past. We bring you something new, something not blue - and you run from it.TEDDYI'm going to strike out on my OWN!OSCARThree strikes and you're out. We have the Umpires - that comes later, though. Around the game plan level. Brinksmanship, edge of the world stuff - you know, like the green candies. The spirit-u-lean-a on-a. Lean-a On-a Me-a. The happy healthy horseshit.

TEDDYI will reveal your true plan to THE WORLDOSCARBut we ARE the world. You're preaching to the choir.TEDDYYour saucer Ruses!! You cannot just come in here and STIR THINGS UP!OSCAR(a big ladle appears in his hands)I think I already HAVE.

INT. DAY. GWEN'S ROOM.

TEDDY

You got Religion? That old list of para-popstars? Your virtual groupie wish-list?

MARONG WTEWART

You can have your SHOW all lyou want - show ME the money1 we are only here for their filthy lucre - that which drives the Big Top - the MARKS-WE WILL STRIP THEM of all their possessions - with the saucer shell game

Like the best way to take over the world is take over the media 0 0the media of exchange --

TEDDY
But that's not possible - we need money - the system the planet
Pay bills - do the KakaBank usury dance - it won't work

OSCAR
We offer total abundance - if you can shake free of your old system!

TEDDY
You're pretty demanding - like an energy vulture. I owe I owe so off to work I go.

SONG: "In The Evening" Zeppelin"

OSCAR
What's life? - to pay bills -That's you counter strategy? Open a luncheonette in the middle of nowhere? Wait for the end of the world?

TEDDYKeep taunting me. Go right ahead. You'll see.OSCARSee what?TEDDYThere are people here! People who care about the future of the world.OSCARYou can have abundance. Why do you choose strife? Cross over here, where it's easiest.I am your Best Buddy!

TEDDYI don't TRUST you.

OSCAR

I thrive on confrontation. I am whatever you want me to be. Adversary. Friend. Lover of your ex.

TEDDYYou are making a MOCKERY of me!OSCARYou're doing fine by yourself.OSCAR/ Fred Astaire light-foots it around in a dancing circle, his trinket-laden belt jangling, the amulet shining.OSCARDo you wanna dance? Under the moonlight, the serious, dangerous moonlight. Do I have a chance? Do you think I'm going places or have I already ARR-ived alive?TEDDYJust what the hell ARE you?OSCAR(his eyes turn coal black - in a grotesque comic voice he says)I am Lucifer.TEDDYYou are?
OSCARAnd you are running from your Fate.TEDDYI'll run. I'll run all night! I'll go with the devil, you bet. For sure!I will RUN for OFFICE.

ADELLE sings ballad-Rap-Up

IT'S ALL LOVE
Please tell me of love - say something from your heart that isn't just filled
with annoyance -It's a dance - the music and feeling are rocking and
reelingInside of meYou must know by now just why and howI really love you
-And it's all Love -

SOUND CUT:

Windows vamp SEQUENCE:Four-tone WINDOWS introduction tone, amplified
symphonicly. Making the connection.

INT. DAY.BARRY and SHIELA wake to see a new Estate II computer on the
table in their bedroom.SHIELASo - that's the new computer. In the middle of
the night. Like the tooth fairy.SUBJECTS download an "upgrade" which links
them into the ALIEN$' Marong Stewart Money System via the ESTATE II
DEVICE -CELL MAGNET - pulls back in - toward the "hub" -INT. TEDDY'S
GROUNDFLOOR CONDO - PEORIAOSCAR at the door. TEDDY answers.OSCAR
in robe and with towel - oversized bar of soap.OSCARShower number 69 is
now ready.TEDDYWhat do you want?OSCARYour wife. Mars needs
women.TEDDYI don't appreciate this.OSCAR holds up the mesmirizing
amulet which stuns TEDDY. Frozen, he stands there, as OSCAR goes in.INT.
GWEN & TEDDY'S BEDROOM. NIGHT.GWEN is lying in her bedroom. Reading
a spinning MagaDisk. The images and text make patterns on her face as she
scrolls through the contents. The Estate II on the nightstand runs through a
series of news images, asking for attention with soft whimpers, like a
lovelorn pet.OSCAR (as TEDDY) comes up behind her.The long rays of light
are crossing the wall slowly. Gwen is in bed spinning her MEGADISC.The
colors of the sequences show on her face.OSCAR(to himself)Now for some
afternoon delight!

GWENYou're not Teddy. You're not my husband.OSCAR(to himself)Back in
the saddle again.OSCARI want to reconcile and consumate.GWENYou talk
like that - alien. Everything robo-speak.The heart of the mystery which is at
the heart of creation is woman.I am your lover.(Teddy/OSCAR in unison)We
are your lovers.

OSCAR
This is a Very SACRED moment - our bodies are joined - we are exchanging
energies -

We are One and in Contact with the Universe - bringing in all downloads.

TEDDY/OSCAR
Ahhhhhhhhh!

He cannot maintain shape change after the orgasm. TEDDY morphs back into OSCAR.

GWEN sees this.
GWEN
You're not my husband. You're not TEDEDY!!!
OSCAR(eyes gleaming)I am - we are your husband.

GWEN
You Beast!

(MS taking the place of OSCAR taking the place of TEDDY)
OSCAR
Six Six Six you're all so sick sick sick No beasdt here. What you NEED is evolution beyond your war-torn global mentality.

NT. NIGHT. THE SAUCER SMOKING AREA.

BILLIs it live or is it Memorex?RODNEYHuh?BILLAn old ad - copy. From the recording days. Before digital. When things were analog.ALTONWhat's that?BILLWe're not looking for tunas with good taste - we're looking for tunas that taste good - yea - that's it - that's what they're after.RODNEY

What

BILLOur essence, Our basic bullshit essence. Our gullibility - our ability to be motivated - by anything - food, sex, war - so be our worst rubes - our worst MARKS -To believe in OURSELVES !Yea, yea, yea!

RODNEY
You need to take you temperature?

(touches him on the forehead)

EXT. DAY. BRONX.CARL comes out of his sister's brownstone, heading up the street. In the far distance, the saucer can be seen. CARL sees a slim, sexy lady walking down the street. She could have a flag saying "tricks" - CARL follows her -

INT. NIGHT. "LAST ACT" NIGHTCARL WASHINGTONI certainly don't feel compelled to have sex with any of these womens any more. Ican cure myself of my sexual addiction -

I can promote the hell out of this if you like.

Now I do, now that I know my sister and can think about a woman.

OSCAR

.Do you like women?

CARL
What's there not to like?

OSCAR
OK OK OK - NOW

OSCAR

When we play the Empathy Game, we change places, to see how the other sees it.

The STAGE beaks up into opposing areas -

The Game of Musical Chairs - first world, second world, third world, et cetera.

We change places, but we ask, in the territorial game,

WHY?
Most wars are fought over territory. Why change place swhen the only concern is death and destruction.

Territorial imperative. Our technology would make territoril strife obsolete - you could be ANYWHERE you want to be. We don't fight over territory because we are EVERYWHERE.And EVERYWHERE can be EVERY THING!So - where's the PLAN? Let's solve the problems, let's just not go to WAR!DISSOLVE TO: TEDDY at the rally cupoula, surround by his crowd of followers =

TEDDY
THANK YOU. For your vote!

EXTERIOR. THE CAMPAIGN HEADQUARTERS IN KANSAS CITY.

"KANSAS CITY" blares over the loudspeakers as TEDDY prepares his speech, surrounded by MR. WRIGHT CAMPAIGN workers.

Banner stretched across the front of the large glass storefront:

WE CAN WORK TOGETHER TO WORK IT OUT AND MAKE IT WORK AND MAKE IT WRIGHT!

Plane flys in like a crop duster - wing acrobatics - heading toward:

KANSAS. FLATLAND. NEAR NEWROUTE 66.ADELLE and TEDDY campaign from a small-town bandstand in the center of a town green surrounded by the desolation of flat land and fields.

BILL, SHIELA, BARRY, RODNEY, ALTON, FARO, FOSS fan out in a triangular pattern from the bandstand.OVERHEAD ANGLE

Outline fo the cell magnet ove rtheir heads, stirring up the response.

Roads radiate out from the center in emulation of the pattern of aisles in the saucers.Cars are parked around the bandstand. There are tables set up with food, barbecue pits smoking with ribs and chicken.

TEDDY
(the new Obama)
A chicken in every pot. A saucer in every driveway.

Why don't we just acknowledge their precious material existence, their influence on our lives, and let them all work for our enjoyment, and have both sides just acknowledge the wealth of beauty, which already exists and continues to be built into the world.

GWEN (VAMPISH)So - territorial. It's all sex. You're just frustrated.Fight or flight. Right?TEDDYWe will get the evil doers behind the Estate II!GWENOh - Who's horny today? Freud said it - all was isrepressed sexuality.Even the saucers draw on that to get their – response

TEDDYWe could deny territoriality, change places with our enemies. That would give everyone a chance to see how the other half lives.
But why change places when the only concern is death & destruction?D&D?

In most minds, sex and death are the nexus of creation.FAROToo liberal for me.TEDDY
ME Tarzan. Me want to open a bar called religion and politics.
GWENA
 fight every night - guaranteed.

GWEN and TEDDY in Duet

"The wind upon my face, I see the sun standing in place, all Time is gone what can I do - I still feel my love for you -”

GWENWhat was our lecture last night? Someone stuck a goddamn coat hanger up her gd asss

-DISSOLVE TO:
TEDDY and ADELLE - "IN THE SPACE BETEEN ACTS" -

"HORSEHEAD NEBULA"The evening is One to RememberYour eyes are like the stars up aboveIt's just one of those clear days in SeptemberAnd I just fell headfirst into LoveAnd the stars are like Sirens beckonningThe Milky Way looks like an open doorIf there is a God then maybe he will love usFor loving in his Image and then come more...The star are like Sirens beckoningThey pull us up and take our fears awayIf I were an astronaut or a geniusI could put it down this wayThe spatial geometry of our meetingIs driftin through the cosmosphereI just found the dimensions of life that are sad and

fleetingJust took a 360 degree turn to the nearThe Horsehead Nebula are shiningShining somewhere out in spaceAnd when we get back to the eveningWe'll find that we have just found our place
SAUCER STAGES (REPRISE)I feel the pulse of the universeThe star studded mystery that we're all part ofComing back to the point of ContactGiving without thought of getting backWhat are you going to do?What are you going to do?What are you going to do?INTERIOR. NIGHTTIME. THE OFFICES OF THE NYLA TIMES.DAK WILLARD sits at a computer terminal, word-processing his review of The Show.On the TV monitor is seen coverage of the TEDDY WRIGHT CAMPAIGN FOR A TOTALLY WRIGHT FUTURE.DAK follows the stock market on another monitor. MARONG STEWART crawls by, showing a huge volume of trading and a spurt on price on the graph.DAK finishes the review on the screen (we see some of it as he edits, over shoulder) and presses the SEND button on the console, gets up for coffee.DAK walks to the coffee machine, fills his cup. He passes the EDITOR's office (Lou Grant type) pausing.
EDITOR
HOW DID IT GO?
DAKThe review? Good, you'll like it.EDITORI monitored it in copy edit. Nothing special. Is the review as complete as it can be?DAKI ran out of notes.EDITORTHERE ARE ALWAYS MORE NOTES.DAKWhat are you driving at?EDITORIt seemed unfinished.

DAK
Who can say. Who can say when The Show is finished, or when its impact can be properly evaluated.
EDITORI have a suggestion.The CELL MAGNET infolds toward the EXITS, passing over the audience heads,

DETAIL: The cup melts in DAK's hand. The walls of the office become indistinct. The outside streets and cars, other buildings, can be seen through the walls. The office breaks up into component lines.The editor turns into OSCAR, as we watch. All but his face then fades, leaving his grinning, leering face, like the Cheshire Cat.
OSCAR'S VOICE
Put aside your considerations. Go back to the Show. Experience it directly.

DAK begins to MELT, TO be pulled "back" into the saucer. We see the shape of the CELL MAGNET behind him, "beaming" him back to his seat.OSCARNOW GET BACK! GO!In ancient Egypt they'd put a person on the table, with two masks on, and weight their soul. Then they'd decide if that body was worth preserving after death. King Tut, now - He had a girlfriend.GWENA mummy.INTERIOR. SAUCER. NIGHT.OSCAR drops from the overhead console.The CELL MAGNET moves around the saucer interior.OSCAR ("PA" VOICE)DID YOU ABSORB THAT?(pause)NOW:QUESTION:WHY DOES HUMANITY DENY ITS POTENTIALFOR PERFECTION BY DESTROYING ITS CAPACITYFOR LOVE, TRUST, AND TOTAL EVOLUTION.Let's answer that -- from you. Tellus, tell the Cell Magnet.The CELL MAGNET sweeps the audience. There is silence.OSCARIt comes down to relating the individual to the universal.SPOTS UP on stage In the CENTER STAGE, there are TEDDY and OSCAR.OSCARWhat is it with these Earth Women?TEDDYYou tell

me.OSCARLike aliens. They can't make a plan, or if they do they can't stick to it.TEDDYLotsa screws loose, just getting worse in this decade.OSCARYou must move forward from Source and know yourself for what you are.People mumbling, barely in control of their language, doing the muddling thing. We call it doing the food thing, the car thing, the sleep thing, the sex thing - whatever. We love you- don't you get it?There is No such Thing as an Alien. You are the Aliens - contact YOURSELVESWe do confrontation first, after Entertainment, then the New Selves, then the Lottery, then the Sharing and Bonding.You see, there is more to the Saucer Lottery than just who gets IN - it's about who gets OUT! Haha.It costs $500 to get in, it costs your life to get out - we will serve no wine before its time - YOU GOT IT?CENTRAL CONSOLE READOUTLIES, DENIAL, MANIPULATIONTheater of Being -TEDDYSO where are they?OSCARAll, oh, back in the - saucer. Probably sleeping a good sleep, while we project out here.They're be ready for the next Show and the Finale.TEDDYThe finale? So we're all just - what did you call them - the virtual people -Your replacements - avatars.OSCARYea, so like it doesn't count, really. We are always COUNTING on the audience.Hope you'll be there. You'll like it - I know.TEDDYSimulated people - in a fake reality. No - I'll pass.Just try to get me there.OSCARYOUR FRIENDS ARE CLOSE - your enemies are even closer! Give me a cigarette.TEDDYNOBARRY MORGAN'S OFFICEBILLCrap. They took over our economy with those computers. Took the Infonet, called it their own.We could create wealth and value but instead we just make money. Like a print run.
Nobody has ever made me THAT money like the aliens and their SHOW.Never before.

MARTHAThe aliens are obviously pushing the envelope of our cherished beliefs - and what we're used to. They're upsetting the apple and the orange cart.
INT. THE SAUCER.

GATES OPENED.THE AUDIENCE files back in.OSCAR on the central stage module.OSCARAND SO ON WITH THE SHOW!

ALIEN BAND gathers with alien-looking guitar, bagpipe and flute-like instruments

SONG:h 1-2-3-4-WHY?

OSCAR
Traveling to planets at the speed of thought.This universe is the only one we got.I know I'll show you what is below you.You know I'll show youWhat is below you and what is not.OSCARThere IS a game - in which YOU are the only PLAYER -so go create your game, WAKE UP, and WIN!BIG BUSBY BERKELEY-like SHOW-stopper number. A DNA ring of DANCERS spiraling around the central VAN DER GRAFF generator float-cake set. LIGHTS gleaming and pinpointing around the saucer interior.SPINNING STAGE - "HUMAN RACE"Why change places, when the only concern is Death and DestructionSex mixed with Death in most minds is the Nexus of

Creation.Your mind is one with the UniverseAnd the Universe is All One.Take the Blinders off Wake Up and Win

BATHROBE SCENE - Tedy, Gwen, OSCAR

MARY-JOSEPH-GOD triangleYou're WHAT? With WHO?

Archangel Michael-Gabriel - with the tanslucent form, the chakra colrs, the pouning heart -

OSCAR
Greetings. If you really love me leave the money on the dresser

ADELLE
Pure Thought People
They know the ways of the waves
Days of bonomo bones and taffy teeth
Inner light illuminating a pounding heart

Pure Thought people put heir toes in a sidewalk crack
To be sure of getting back

INT. THE BEAMSHIP BAR - NIGHT

OSCARI am now and have always been the ONE and you are the OUtSIDER looking IN.

TEDDY
Look in the mirror, green-brains. Who's the fairest of them all?
You are only talking to yourself. I am the MIRROR of you - your earth-self

OSCAR
You are PREGNANT with POSSIBILITY
I see that - that is why I wanted to -- - help you and Gwen
I have many children - If I get the time - I never see them You are now pregnant with possibility - do something

TEDDY
The psychotic always attempts to balance itself. Not being on galactic net is like having only half of my brain. Your son - your Sol - is creating sunspot interference - shit happens - Shyte goes to the Little Green People - help me help your planet - I hope you have a son and call him Sol -Got Sol-utions?

OSCAR
This is a cover - we put on bodies the way you put on clothes -The simplest alien form, the vacuous eyes, featureless torso, big head, you know - that's the purest form of the basic lifeform sensory cluster - what you see is what you get -This is the way I really look - I'd show you more but I wouldn't want to blind you -GWEN sees the svelte Casanova Don Juan alien slips away and be replaced by a translucent figure 3'4" tall, translucent, whose heart interior can be seen pumping and pounting a green fluid, then back to the

"handsome" alienGWEN-TEDDY-OSCAR events leading up to im-concept via alienThe screensOSCAR and SHIELA.OSCARYou are facing some of your fears - that is good.INTERIOR. THE COMPUTER-COPY-SHARE STOREOSCARSome of you are still ostracized from yourselves. You are the aliens, you are the alienated. You are separated from your being and not certain of your future. This you must change for the Present.Let me show you.In all reference-cutaway shots the ARRAY of TV monitors in the dept store windows represent the BODY PUBLIC, the WORLD POV, the concept of humanity at-large. The FACES of HUMANITY.Central Console:INT. THE SAUCER - CONTRAYOR SECTION.FARO is rematerialized out of the half-circle of the matter-translator and slides down the contrayor with the same momentum he had on the bar in the previous scene. He scatters more bottles and collides with DRINKERs sitting on the contrayor belt.OSCARFollow the drinking gourd, now, gumbaya!He blows a whistle.OSCAREverybody out of the gene-pool Follow me. Bunny hop. Lindsey six! Onward March.Line dancing, lady's choice! Ooo la la.OSCAR draws a line with his walkng stick behind him. LIGHTS dim.Illuminated PAC-MAN like GLOBES bounce ahead, lighting the way in the bar-gloom dark.Now drunk, the audience follows the Saucer Program into

INT. THE SAUCER. "THE SHARING"
The SUPERSEATS swivel so that the AUDIENCE MEMBERS face each other.OSCARWho are you afraid you are? Who are you afraid to be?Face that person and become what you really are, so the other person across from you can be your guide. We may be sitting next to our own personal savior and now know it;.Remember: there is no such thing as an "alien."

BILL
I remember everything -- that's the problem -

The "EMOTIONAL LANDSCAPE" of the participants, blending face-2-face, is displayed on the screen.INTERIOR - glowing, pounding heart - "Fantastic Voyage" through the inner body, up to the brain - the "emotional landscape" is Dali-like, populated byADELLEI rely on you. I need you.BILLWe deliver images to a world that needs them.ADELLEHow can people live next to each other and not LOOK at each other.SUPERSEATS turn so that each audience member is facing another.OSCARMr. Faro Constantinople, manof the world!FARO is surrounded by a "hall of mirrors" (more like a screen ofmirrors, like dressing screens -- no man a hero to his valet,etc.) The "screens" show scenes of his brutality.OSCARYou have a heart of gold beneath that.You love your mother.So, why do you hurt?FARONo one was ever good to me. I didit all myself.OSCARBut surely you loved -- someone.FARONOOSCARYour father.FAROMy father was like me.OSCARYou loved my mother.FAROShe raised me. She never rested.OSCARYou are a spiritual man, a seer.FAROSometimes.OSCARWhy do you avoid what you can doFOR the world?FAROI don't know.OSCARYou can do so much good - what isyour sense of good?.FAROI can use my vision to achievepower. I can get what I want.CELL MAGNET shows CLOSEUPS of audience faces, POV.OSCARShare.BIFFWhat's this, human potential?OSCARIt's whatever you say it is.(Blinking)Nobody going to tell me I need to shave.CLOSE ON TEDDY looking over the rainbow field. LOOKING with anticipation as the "JERUSALEM SHIP" manevers for landing, so they can get on board the Galactic Ark.(blinking)BARRYI was at the doctor's the other day - he was doing a rectal exam - had the 'scope up my rear end - said "you wanna take a look" - so I looked, and you know what? I'm a beautiful asshole.FAROI'm horney. Fat, successful, powerful, ten wives, and I have too much going on. I'm horney for life, for love, for simplicity, to be part of the universe.OSCARThe assurance that the universe is One and you are a part of the Universe - that is what all living beings seek. You are "part of the whole."THE CELL MAGNET circles overhead.INT. MARONG STEWART OFFICE. NIGHT.A THOUSAND display saucer faces contorted in pain or joy. THE CELL MAGNET pulls out personal pains and joys,INT. SAUCER."NIGHT" MUSIC ON TRACK: PACHABEL CANON SUITEDISPLAY ON CONSOLE: some of the face details.THE LAYING ON OF HANDSThe bodies of the participants begin revolving on the contrayor. The OTHERS put their hands on EACH OTHER, feeling the shapes of the OTHERS' bodies, as they pass by.FLOATING.Adelle lies on the conveyor system, nude. She then begins revolving around the circle.The hands-on begins.USHERADELLE weeps silently as she is carried aloft by the participants. OSCAR scans the people all around.Other bodies are lifted by the participants, floated, then put on the conveyor system. As they revolve around so much human meat, the hands are laid on them by the other participants.The faces should reflect this near-Godlike beatitude fully with Rembrant-esque lighting from below-eye-level lighting from the conveyor system's illumination.INTERIOR. THE SAUCER. SAUCER HOLOGAME.The 3-D SPACEGRID GAME appears in the central stage area. A central score console lights up with the PLAYERS' names.A 3D interactive space invaders game. The invaders are - ourselves. OSCAR emerges on stage.BRAN CANow you get to play Space Invaders for real. It is your own space.The SUPERSEATS swivel back on their mounts.The helmet-glasses descend over the faces of the participants.OSCARGrip your control sticks and prepare to fire.OVERHEAD, a game field appears, in three dimensions. Simulcra of audience members appear overhead (it is usually one's companion, or Significant Other) - their projections appear as 3D targets, dropping toward the audience. People face what they most fear about their human mirrors - their friends and lovers. What they can't say, do, or be.In some cases, it is themselves, or other people from the Projections.Audience members vanish, drawn up into the central console of the CELL MAGNET digitizer. Then, friends, mates, loved-ones begin descending out of the master projector, in 3D, descending toward their opponents in the seats.GWEN sits in her seat. Overhead, TEDDY appears. ANGLE, from her POV, looking through the chair sights at TEDDY, whose 3-D image is dancing in space, coming in toward her.SHIELAThis is for the mortgage, This is forall the money you've pissed away on booze!She fires and destroys a floating deed, a cluster of whisky bottles descending from the central image generator.GWENThis is for all those empty nights at home while you cruised the bars. This is for my feeling of emptiness!GWEN bursts the TEDDY-figure. She explodes the image of people laughing at a bar. A shattering sound and cries of pain, speeded up and fading.FARO aims at his domineering father. At his helpless, weak, luxury bound mother. He destroys them both, They emerge, loving him.FARO'S M/FWe love you boy! Our son!

MARGIE's BOSS appears corning out of right field.

BAN!The billcollector appears above. ZAP! Gone in a stroke of blue light. He reappears above, descending toward

CARL.

COLLECTOR
YOU MUST PAY THE RENT.

ZAP!

THE OMEGA POINT = Merging of the Material and Spiritual planes

CENTRAL CONSOLE: HERE COME EVERYBODY!

The bodies now being circled aroun on the conveyer system. Stunned, they circle immobile while the audience members who have remained seated lay their hands on their bodies.

EXT. LARGE VIEW. NIGHT SKY.

VIEWPOINT: Above the earth. The saucers dance in a grand circle, all 128 (10%) of them glowing intensely through a pattern of colors.INT. NIGHT.THE saucer rises above the earth. Dance of saucers, merging and separating.The participants now float in zero-G. The floating and laying of hands continue. Weightless love, with no friction.SPARKLES of light exchange between saucers in formation. Changing of hues. Crystaline light formations. Hues glisten through changes of light frequency.VIEWPOINT: From below, saucers are seen in a flying pattern, in cartwheels, loops, fleur-de-lis, dying-swan dives, regrouping in a central cluster, returning to earth, splitting off to return to their locations.INT. SAUCER.Weight is returned. The glowing conveyor system delivers fruit and wine to the audience.It is HAPPY HOUR aboard the saucer.People drink, laugh, talk. The saucer is a bar. The contrayors are bar surfaces. Beer signs, hard liquor product promotions dangle around the audience members.A festive, party mood is suddenly upon the groups.USHERS circulate among the audience members in their superseats, with trays, change holders, order pads.Would you like to order?OSCAR, GWEN and ADELLE grouped in a seating cluster, on either side of the contrayor.OSCARNot just now, thanks.Troops gather just beyond the lights, all around the stage. The INQUISITION stage revolves around onto the stage, filled with audience members.CENTRAL CONSOLE:The cultural objects & artifacts are piled in a huge pile for a bonfire inside the saucer.DETAIL: Faces warmed by the red light of the fire as their culture burns.OSCARYour house is burning!EXT. SPACE.FADE-DISSOLVE TO:DANCE OF SAUCERS IN SPACECLOSEOSCAR's eyes fill with tears, looking on...THE LAYING ON OF HANDSDISSOLVE TO:TEDDY in a TRUCK STOP on the road.PA (LOUD)Shower number 486 is now ready. Shower number 666 is now ready. Shower number 133 is NOW READY.TEDDYI trusted you with my wife - should I trust you with my life?OSCARIn bother cases I maintained them - didn't I. Maintained and supported.More than you could do at times.TEDDYThat's a whole other matter.OSCARMatter and time - it don't matter if I don't have time.TEDDYSo - it could go either way.OSCARYou could make a difference - or a distance. Not having you - completely - within the Show, 100% - that is --It is like a wound, which will not heal.TEDDY(angry now)You must have me mistaken for someone who gives a shit. You must think I'm some kind of card.OSCARYou are - worth playing. In the ultimate game. Chose it, make the words express it, make it yours. What you want - wife? A new life? What do you see in the cards?TEDDYMore pain. More manipulation. More of your saucer games. Marong Stewart - you are afraid of Marong Steewart, because Marong Stewart IS you. You other half, your dark side.

OSCAR
Your trouble with communicating totally your desirous energy thwart; evolution and use of total personalities and global potentials. We have sublimed our energies and refined our drives. The sex drive is the space drive. Your puritanical culture, and separation of procreation and romance, has given never-ending headache. You could not accept the connection between drive and the space drive, the raw sexual drive and the need to be created. Remorse for the human race? Maybe it's time. YOU WOULD NOT GET IT.
CENTRAL CONSOLE
PROCESSENIUM ARCH - THE ARK OF THE CHARACTERS

HOLOGAMEOSCARGrab your control sticks and PREPARE TO FIRE!The seats tilt upward, toward the scroll-work dome of the saucer interior.OBJECTS and PEOPLE begin to manifest, high above, descending fast, toward the individual participants.INT. THE SAUCER. "NIGHT" SUBJECT: "DEMONSTRATION OF TOTAL POWER."SUPER ON SCREEN: JUNE 2014INT. THE SAUCER. NIGHT.OSCARYOU HAVE -- ALL OF YOU -- BEEN LOOKINGAROUND FOR SOMETHING RIGHT IN FRONT OF YOU----That's each other!YOU can go into the universe -- you can find the stars -- it's in your genes -- it's in the mind of the universe -- just release that mind into your own stream of action -- you can find the right way!GWENI have needs - you have needs.OSCARYea, we have an agreement. A covenant.GWENThat's not love - that's expediency.OSCAROr they're just young.GWEN unsure of OSCAR's non-sequiter.OSCARConscious evolution is an act of self-discovery, or faith. Is it that hard to understand & appreciate that what is, just IS?

GWEN
Yes.

OSCAR
I know you and your planet intimately. And we have only been here a few months.

GWEN
It's your faith in US, right?

OSCAR
Love leads to understanding.Every religious system contains an evolutionary leap from the physical to the universal.GWENI don't know about that.

OSCAR
You will -- when you make the leap.

GWEN

TO THE UNIVERSAL

Consciousness is the point and the objective of this interplanetary exercise.

OSCAR
I am now since the beginning of time and shall forever be The OneYou're just
out to get us.,

OSCAR
Get you in the right way - get you involved in a universe beyond your
immediate game-playing.Universal spirit is the art of belief. We don't get
mad -- we get even.

OSCAR joins them in virtual space.

TEDDY
I always knew that paradise was right in front of me. I always wondered why
couldn't see it -GWENI knew it was there but I just couldn't say it.TeddySay
it. NOW.OSCARYOU HAVE -- ALL OF you -- been looking around for
something right in front of you!YOU can go into the universe, YOU can find
the stars -- it;s in your genes -- it's in the mnind of the Universe...just
release that mind into your own stream of action -- you can find the right
way!TEDDYDays of delight. Control of our own
destiny.OSCARChoice.OSCARAgain, you have been looking for something
that is right in front of you -- there is your path to the Universe. Each
other.TEDDYDays of delight -- control of our own destiny.GWENWho told you
I was pregnant?OSCARYou have been looking for something which is right in
front of you -- there is your path to the Universe.

MARKEE: OSCAR'S CAFE GALAXYOSCAROut of all the two-bit late night bars
in the universe, the dame has to walk into mine.BEER KEGS ROLL ONTO THE
STAGE
OSCAR in toga guiding the drinkersOSCARLet's not see each other any
more.GWEN
No - I'm supposed to say that. I'm the one who does the "Dear John" around
hereWOMANIs that the ugliest shirt you could findMANWant to know what I
really think?I think you are the ugliest person - you are a fat-assed bitch
who annot do anything except invade the space of three nice guys who are
ENJOYING their late-night meal -WOMANWhile you're out here getting drunk
with your buddies, how long do you think she'll stay at home waiting - not
never - no -DAK goes into the basement of the tenement brownstone. There
the BROTHERS are playing dice. In the corner CARL is toking up on a crack-
pipe, and in the shadow of the corner a GIRL is giving his brother sexual
service.CARLHey man get out of here - we don't have no space for no lily-
livered white oldster.

GWENYou ARE crazy. Alien.OSCARNo - c-Wazy! (spluttering) I AM super SILLY- ous.He hops around one leg with the other, like Curly of the Three Stooges.This is cupidity!

OSCARDownload from the universe!(Sucking sound as he saises his hands above his head, reverse-grip)

EXT. DAY. COLORADO SPRINGS. THE GOVT COMMUNICATIONS NEXUS - MICROWAVE FACILITY.TEDDY drives a beat-up pickup truck through the mountains. The large saucer next to the main relay is totally Stealth-black, huge and foreboding.

The Central saucer Unit.
EXT. SPACE.EYE PATTERN to SPIRAL VORTEX, MULTI COLOR DOWN TO:STREET LEVEL: CONCRETE.TEDDY's view of the street, from his position on the hardtop, face down.WHAT HE SEES:EXTERIOR. DOWNTOWN PEORLA. (LIKE LA BY THE BUS STATION)TEDDY's face against the surface of the street. A burning barrel in the background. Looming shape of saucer, further background.TEDDY rises with difficulty.Pull back from main FOUNTAIN of a circular motief, the DisEnfranchised sitting around. Background, there is a food kitchen setup, scooping out chili and bread for the stragglers.Everywhere, up and down the streets, tents with people in them - TEDDYThrown out.TEDDY huddles with the others around the burning barrel.OVERHEAD, the ghostly outline of the saucer interior and CELL MAGNET.DETAIL: OSCAR'S FACE PULL BACKDISSOLVE IN PULL BACK TO: His viewTO:OSCAR is there, in the background, dressed as a bum, watching his minions, waiting in line for food. His eyes speak, as he blinks them rapidly.

CLOSE ANGLE ON TEDDY, others clustered around the burning barrel.TEDDYDepression.FOSSPsycological AND economic.And I'm an ecopsycologist - without a marketRODNEYThrown out of paradise -- out of -- the saucer.FAROFor the sin of not relating! What is that?THE OSTRACISED huddle around a burning barrel. Loud punk rock music blares from a warehouse nearby.EXTERIOR. DAY,FARO (DRUNK)FARO has no money And I -- thirsty too.CLOSE, FARO. He uses an overlarge fountain as a water bubbler, hopping down the other side, looking for places to scavange for food. He is a big man.

INTERIOR. NIGHT. A RESTAURANT

FARO runs in and scoops up the plates of those who have just eaten, before their leftovers are taken to the trash.FAROHungry!EXTERIOR, NIGHT.FARO walks the streets by the docks, a threadbare coat, smoking a rolled cigarette. Bums accost him. He looks up to se a huge supertanker looming above the pier. It is the CELL MAGNET in the shape of a boat.

Sign: (CENTRAL CONSOLE): LOCKOUT/ NO UNION.FARO carries a large canvas sea bag over his shoulder.FARO"All that I have in the world now in this bag - papa's got a brand new bag - "Two YOUTHS try to grab it from him. He kicks at them; they run away, jeering.YOUTHYouYou bum!DISSOLVE to bar where FARO drinks. Rolling around the place, he accosts others.FAROHey, baby, I'll vote for you! Put a bag over your head and any guy would do it.He leers, belching.FARODo you know who I am? Iowned the entire fleet! FARO slides down the contrayor on his belly, scattering objects.The WOMAN backs away. FARO holds up his hands.FAROBoats! Big boats!PROPRIETOR comes up to him.FAROI own the whole damn fleet!PROPYou're just another drunk, buddy!OPERATIC VOLUME OF ALIEN SOUND.FAROIs this phase one of lumpy gravy?ALTONAre you afraid of me? You want to get some beer? I know houses where they are looking out the windows. You want to make some money with that pen?Excuse me for being in the way.It's not your fault - it's the architecture.

OSCARWoke up this early AM dreaming of my first galactic girlfriend who appeared as your Earth Mother Mary -- so tranquil so serene.People will respond that which reminds them of states beyondMoney. Life states this. - Ask anyone from the depression what was the least depressing aspect of it - it was "life" itself. And people went to the movies a lot. We know - we've been monitoring your radio and television for decades.
There are a million things going in global reality besides fretting over the change or the tax on an amount. We waste a lot of time working with the money system – need to go to Books A Million and look at a million stars

TEDDY
Amateur Aliens

TEDDYAnything goes.OSCAR"Getting to know you, getting to know all about you..."OSCAR lifts the bottle, drinking - points at TEDDYOSCARTheory: Versus. Reality.You cannot be creating if your are only "doing money" - the is the lessonof bad art and "suits." Life lives in the cracks between the motion of money.

A BIG ALIEN SEX OBJECTWOrLD tAKEOVer thiNg

IT'S A RAP IN THE RAP

CIRQUE DU SOLEIL IN SPACE

A metronic system, you are understanding the waves, the valence nature of exchange.TEDDYI have no idea what you just said.OSCARIt is a field. Stop me if I'm going too fast for you.Money comes in to fill in & make executable the spaces "creativity" createswith workable ideas.Then it becomes a System, which often then needs redoing.But how many change it?TEDDYI don't know - how many? Jesus, I was just trying to make a buck.OSCARA few. The prophets, the visionaries. Aha! See there, your Programed to think it is difficult, just like your entire planet is pre-Programmed for the doomsday or the Great Comeuppance.

END SIDEBARINT. NIGHT. WASHINGTON, D.C. TEDDY WRIGHT'S CONSUMER HOTLINE OFFICEA circular conference table, evoking the War

Room of Dr Strangelove, or the Stonehenge array. A central recording pylon looks like the central "probe" of a radio dish telescope.RODNEYWe're fucked.Close, STENO, typing.TEDDYPlease strike that. Be more specific. Make it simpler.ALTONWhat he means is -- we're the New Age, and they're into making slaves -- info- slaves.TEDDYThat needs to be proved.ALTONLook at it this way -- Marong Stewart blows into town and set up -- a marketing wing -- to install the brain computer --

TEDDY
Yea.ALTON

Now think of it -- if this is the aliens' own alter ego -- their dark side -- then they are going to be their own worst enemy --

RODNEYLet's put it this way -- if I wantedto live forever, I'd be a corporation.
They are treated like people -- plus granted limited liability for major disaster -- like stripping the atmosphere, destroying plankta, or taking over the economy to wipe it out --

TEDDY
The New World Order. RODNEYVe vas only following ORDERS.ALTONNo order - only chaos.INNER LANDSCAPE --
"THROUGH THE EYES" TEXTURE MAP INTERIORThe emotional landscape, the past of a person's experiences displayed as a phantasmogoric landscape, literally "each individual is and entire world/ and entire Universe." Measuring EQ - emotionbal quotient.MORONGTOWN-A GREAT TOWN TO GROW WITH, incorporating: STEWARTVILLE, a Delaware city in IllinoisSTEPFORD wives go back and forth to stores, cars, markets. Like CELEBRATION at Orlando Disney 192.

BARRY
There is not politics. There is only economics!

Menu Options

It's

INTERIOR. THE SAUCER. CELL MAGNET POV.The CELL MAGNET fast pans over the audiece heads, making stops on faces, zooming in.STOP ONECARL WASINGTONI want to succeed! I want to rise above!SAMWhat good is it to be a good man? Youwork hard, your wife takes up withanother man -- what's that?STOP TWOOSCAREvery day when you go out you miss the opportunity to relate, to bring the together.One thing I could not stand about yourCity New York was that everyone avoid thesimple truth of the being next to them.STOP THREECARLYea, tell me about New York. Harlem. The ghetto. I wanted to get out. But there is power to keep you there.STOP FOURBILLI'd come home at night -- working hard. I'd want nothing more than to hold her, touch her, she wouldn't be there for me!OSCARHow can you go on avoiding?STOP FIVEMARTHAHe was so angry, so success driven!He wouldn't really talk to me!BILLWhat can you say?BRAN CASilence is adequate.OSCAR stands center stage, his ideogram of Purpose gleaming. The CELL MAGNET sweeps the audience.INT. NIGHT. THE SACUER.CLOSE, OSCAR.BRAN CAIgnatius Foss, come on down!No!FOSSOSCARYes -- you're part of The Show.FOSS is lifted and flung down to the stage by the CM GRAVITY BEAM.The Audience Participants begin singingWE WANT OUR MONEY BACK choral style.We want our money back...we want our money back -We didn't like the Show, we want our money back -So we can GO -- We want our money back -INT. THE SAUCER CONTROLANGEL 1I've had it. I don't want to spend the rest of infinity on this forsaken rock.Here goes the flop spheres. Take the money and RUN!ANGEL 2Are you sure?ANGEL 1Sure I'm sure. I have a lady half my age waiting for me back at the Hub.I don't want to disappoint her. No flop here, no flop there.SWEEP-WIPE DISSOLVE TO:GWENI want you to be scared. When you take my soul.I'll take that and that and that - put the faces together.TEDDYThey have our faces, you know, digitized - they can replicate us any timeGWENGetting nervous?TEDDYThis is just what we DON't need. Reverse iridology, taking over my brain.GWENAnd soul.GWENI am so lackadazicle. Lazy like a cat. Turn me into a cat, turn me on -this unlnown best that had come out of the world of musicworldOSCAR1-2-3-4-WHY?GWENWoo woo woo wooGWENNight of the VOO-DOOHoo Doo YooooDAKPsycho-sexual revo-evo...and more.OSCARLook at history.SCENE SPIN RESOLVESTO:ROTUNDA, upward shot to overhead scrollwork DISSOLVE TO:INT. THE HALL OF CONGRESS.OSCAR appears behind TEDDY.OSCARGive 'em hell, Teddy!TEDDYI willMake sure to tell them WHOSE CHILD IT IS!TEDDY(still walking)I will!OSCAR(pointing accusingly)That's really smart -- the Anti-Christ is none other than Teddy Wright's little bundle of joy.TEDDYIs none other than Marong Stewart -- YOUR little bundle. Your ALTER little alien ego.OSCAROh, I wouldn't know about that. The world is normal, now, but it still may not work for you...TEDDYWe'll see!OSCARYou can't go on avoiding me forever.TEDDYYou and I are throughOSCAROr just beginningTEDDYNO!TEDDY enters the chamber, takes the podium. The SPEAKER OF THE HOUSE introduces the Congressman from Kansas, Theodore Wright.TEDDYI am speaking tonight to warn youof a most dread force in the land, adanger now facing this country.The force is a Beast in the land. It isforce designed to wipe us out.Create a Hell on Earth,OSCAR(mocking)Turn all freedom-loving people into manipulated slaves.TEDDYThis Beast has in mind a new Dark Ages. The name of who has perpetrated this ignoble confrontation,The Name of the Beast is MARONG STEWART.PANNING SHOTCheers in the hall for the Senator's warning. OSCAR stands.OSCARTell them who fathered the little bastard.TEDDYAnd my solemn promise to you is to leadyou in the battle to end the alien alter-ego!OSCAR/TEDDY:WIPE OUT THISINTERNATIONAL MONSTER WHO WOULD BRINGUS INTO A NEW DARK AGE ON THE EARTH.You have been duly warned. Now is thetime for ACTION.MARONG STEWART MUST DIE!Sound of applause.OSCAR stands applauding the speech. They are alone in the chambers, OSCAR and TEDDY.TEDDY looks up, sees the shape of the CELL MAGNET, shadowy. above their heads, and realizes he is still in the saucer, he never left.OSCARAll audiences are ultimately the one audience.EXTERIOR.The Capitol Building changes into the saucer, with the reflectingpool and trees still surrounding it.EXTERIOR. WASHINGTON. A DAY LATER.LONG TILT up the side of the luxury hotel in which TEDDY stays.TEDDY is in his bathroom of his hotel room. He unrolls the crumpled note OSCAR has written him on the sparkle-paper. TEDDY holds it up to the mirror to read the reverse writing:ARE YOU READY?it says.TEDDY WRIGHT faces the TEDDY WRIGHT SIMULACRUM on the other side of the mirror, the anti-person. His reflection smiles.SIMULACRUMAre you ready?The crystal appears, in the mirror, drawing TEDDY in, to create a simulacra of him in the saucer interior. TEDDY fades into a trance. Standing behind him (in the mirror) is OSCAR, holding the spinning crystal.TEDDY is sucked into the MIRROR and transported to join the others in the simulation of Down Town Depression.OSCARPlaying with you "earth-links" is like playing Saucer Roulette. You don't know what you know, you don't know what you're going to get, so for ten years' time in the future, from 2001 to 20011, I say to you: Who are you , who are you, who are you?

THE MYSTERY AT THE HEART OF CREATION

CUT TO: ELDERS CIRCLEELDERHere go the flop-spheres - no flop THIS show!EXT. NIGHT. "DOWNTOWN PEORIA" (LIKE LA)SFX:"PUNK" ROCK - HEAVY METALFARODepression...TEDDYPsycological AND economic...FARO pulls out his pockets.FAROEmpty. I can't get any money out.DAK"Barrel, barrel burning brightIn the doldrums of the night..."RODNEYHey man, you are DEEP!The INDIGENT, gathered around a burning barrel.TEDDYMarong Stewart got it - all the money - now you gotta be on the grid or you don't exist.Thumbprint, voice ID, hand-eye motion gesture ID.FAROShow me a SIGN!DAK"In Xanadu did Kubla Khan a stately Pleasure-Dome decreeWhere Alph the Sacred River ran through canverns measureless to manDown to a sunless sea..."BARRYWhat the fuck does THAT mean?DAKPoetry. You should read it sometime.BILLI used to.

BARRY
They USED me they used my GREED. And my NEED - to sell these brain-computers. Like MYSOFT.

Now I'm locked out - no upgrades - no product cycles, no future!

Look at this - they got us into the loop and now there's no access - can.t even make a FAQ call - I wanted to send all the messages bulk to the clients but the Program stopped me!

BARRY
Your little programs and gadgets never work !

Get out of my life get out of my wife - I am DONE with the money - I was always working for the MONEY - I didn't know I was destroying my own NATURE

OSCAR

As systems evolve what was once hardware beomes software. The ship is like an elaborate Program. LARGE SIGN on the side of a warehouse.

LOCKOUT/ NO UNIONWHAT DO YOU WANT YOUR INFONET TO BE? NOTHING. NULL SET. THE BEAST OF BURDENTEDDY(tossing aside a cigarette)Must go find that freaking alien.EXT. PEORIA STREET. NIGHT.An illuminated tech store, with hundreds of monitors in the windows. The images of the saucer-sharing are on the TV monitors. Hundreds of faces.

INT. THE PEORIA BLACK-LIGHT BAR.Up on the TV, the interior of the saucer, showing the sitcom party going on in the superseats.

OSCAR throws the switch

BARRY digitized and vaulted out of the Local Scene to COMPUBAR set.

INT. THE SAUCER. NIGHT.

CENTRAL CONSOLE
HAPPY HOUR CENTRAL
CONSOLE READOUT: THE HOUR THAT STRETCHES

FARO, reconstructed by the hemisphere on the CONTRAYOR slides through with the same momentum as in the bar in PEORIA, and slides down the line, scattering glasses, ashtrays.FAROI didn't realize! I didn't realize!PROPRIETOR grabs FARO by the seat of the pants and hurls him into a table. The DRINKERS pick him up and throw him onto the bar. He slides down the length of the bar, scattering bottles.The waiters are two USHERS FARO stumbles through the bar, drunk, accosting people.BARTENDER picks up FARO and throws him down on the bar. He moves down the shiney surface faster than you'd expect. Scatters glasses, ashtrays, etc.At the point where the bar breaks there is a HEMISPHERE which dissolves FRAO's body as he hits it, like a table saw from the side.INTERIOR. SAUCER. "NIGHT"FARO'S POV - sliding down the contrayor, as the saucer spins.He slides by the people who are drinking and laughing. He is propelled along, past DAK WILLARD. FARO hits the hemisphere, is destroyed, broken down...reconstructed through the hemisphere on the other side.DAK(drinking from the force-tube, drunk)That's amazing. They can do the same with life!The BODY of FARO is reconstructed in the same realtime as the dissolution, as he continues down the contrayor surface, scattering the SAUCER BAR service objects, passing by the audience partiers.The PARTIERS are drinking and watching the RICK'S CAFE GALAXY

DAK makes notes in his pad. DAK looks up to see:

ENTROPY SERVICE OFFERED DAILY FOR MONEY-ADAM'S CURSE & EVE'S CURSE

FARO sliding along the Contrayor, scattering the priceless objects the PLAYERS have accumulated from their LIFEGAME.

EXT. DAY. THE BLUFF. RUSE PROJECTION.OSCAR stands on a high bluff overlooking the Pacific Ocean.

TEDDY stands about a hundred yards away from him. Strapped into a hang-glider apparatus. OSCAR raises his arm.

OSCARHave faith, Theodore. You can do it!

TEDDYFaith? You're talking about faith?OSCARYes! That you believe in the universe which contains you and you are also that universe, in this moment, now, and it will SUPPORT you!

TEDDY
Yea, and in what book is that written?

OSCAR
Were you looking for a text, a book to this musical and biological exchange? You need the transition gene - we had to get it into your race somehow. We don't walk in like you think, so easily. This ain't the Big Easy.
Dude.

TEDDY soars in a graceful arc back over OSCAR, climbing in altitude.

TEDDY'S POV
Looking down at the trees, landscape, OSCAR's tiny figure.

OSCAR'S VOICE
Trust me! Teddy, trust me, see? YOU can do it.

OSCAR (TO HIMSELF)The loneliness of the human race at the bottom of the gravity well. The pain of separation. Will it out through the Show.

OSCAR in his beekeepers head covering, with bees swarming INSIDE the hat

OSCAR
No honey, no money -
Come back Teddy! We need you!

EXT. DAY. THE DESERT. THE USED CAR SALES LOT.

Plastic flags flapping and spinning in the strong breeze. An assortment of used cars.

TEDDY walks up to the used car lot.
OSCAR(WITH PENCIL-THIN, BOSTON BLACKIE-STYLE MOUSTACHE)
What can I do you for TWO DAY?

TEDDYI need a car.

OSCAR
What d'ya neeed it for?

TEDDY
I got a ship to meet.
TEDDY
Need to get away, by myself.

OSCAR (VOICE)

I am now and have always been the One

TEDDY
Not for me.

OSCAR
One is All, it it's All Love. A binding force. For you - for your planet. I would show you what I REALLY LOOK LIKE BUT IT WOULD BLIND YOU. A blinding force.

You must come back and complete the show. Otherwise, your planet cannot move on to the next stage of evolution

TEDDYWhy would we need to do that

OSCARBecause staying where you are leads to destruction.

Or: you could have TOTAL abundance and self evolution -You wouldn't want THAT now would you?

TEDDY gets in to start the truck. It does not start. He holds the Payment Book.If I drive it off the lot, it's worth a lot less.OSCAR'S VOICELike your future life if you don't go back to the saucer theater.TEDDY(kicking the tires)I HATE CARS - I HATE CARS!!!

CENTRAL CONSOLE READOUT
ALIEN REVELATION - THERE IS NO ALIEN – WE ARE ALL IN THIS UNIVERSE TOGETHER - CLIMAX AND FINAL COSMOLOGY - \

OSCAR
I am not my money field – repeat after me – I am not my money - I am my Mercaba star-self Spirit

MARTHA
Whatever that is.

BARRY
I AM NOT MY MONEY – I refuse to be limited by the numbers that go with my "finances" - I am not my suit

OSCAR

Especially when playing cards – say again

BARRY
I AM NOT THE MONEY. I AM THE SPIRIT.

OSCAR
We are the aliens – and we are only here FOR the money – so show me the money, show me YOUR money -

BARRY

We are at the end of the loop - I am A bit of a philosopher
We have let the system take over our Humanity - I want to reassert the Humanity in the System!

LONG DAY'S JOURNEY INTO HARD DAY'S NIGHT

SONG: "666 you're so sick sick sick" -- "LIFE, DEATH & THE ORIGIN OF TIME…etc."

Aerial PULL BACK up to showing where Teddy IS ON THE LOT NEXT TO THE ROAD, GOING EAST AND WEST, another going NORTH and SOUTH.

Reaching to both coasts, PULL BACK up through the clouds showing the insignificant DOT where TEDDY has broken down.

TEDDY
My Ship is coming in.

OSCAR
Then don't be at the airport. BE at the space port. Break down to build up - that is the point of evolution, of theater, or the point of contact.Faith, compassion, patience, tenderness.

TEDDY
I'll s-s-show her !

OSCAR
What do you need the car for?

OSCARHow? To save humanity.

OSCARA tall order. By the way, how tall are you? How much legroom do you need? Better yet - how much headroom?OSCAR makes a cupping gesture with his hands above his head, then a slurping sound with his bill-mouth.OSCARI just download all the information I need directly from the universe whenever I need it.TEDDY (NERVOUSLY LAUGHING)Get out of here.OSCARNo - You get out of here - and get BUSY.OSCARLet's look at this one over here.An EXPERIMENTAL jet aircraft, low to the ground, tarnished-burnished, like it has been sitting along time, its cockpit open.OSCARThe keys are in - ready to drive.TEDDY looks at the ship. He is paralyzed, does

not know whether to move forward or back off.OSCARYes, Teddy, go ahead. You CAN DO IT.
EXT. DAY. THE DESERT.They climb into the sky, rolling over.DISSOLVE TO:
EXT. DAY. NO TIME.A huge salt-flat bed. An aircraft testing site.There is a sleek needle-nosed aircraft on the ground, its cockpit open. OSCAR is dressed in test pilot outfit.ANGLE on TEDDY, dressed in the same kind of outfit.OSCAR gestures for TEDDY to get into the front seat, and he gets into the back seat. The cockpit cover descends.EXT. THE LAKE BED.ANGLE on the rocket plane. The engines fire and the ship speeds down the salt bed to takeoff.POV inside the plane as it climbs.REVERSE POV - the trail of jet exhaust as the plane climbs.TEDDY'S POV - the instruments, the joystick, as the plane climbs through the clouds.Audience members WATCH as TEDDY soars up to the "weightless" curve of space.
EXT. THE PLAIN.

THE SAUCER appearing in the desert matrix.
The SAUCER rises, joined by the thousand other saucers in a grandiose complex of saucer flight patterns.
The audience members kick up their feet in a joyous celebration of weightless floating. The saucer climbs toward the stars.

OSCAR

I do not know why you Irth people spend so much time with your money. You must rise ABOVE your money system to truly evolve!

Beware the JUPITER CLASS OF OBJECTS

It's all a mercenary, mercurial MONEY GAME
Are you in the Game? What Game do you Play?

Subroutines in saucer dollars – they took over our media network – are using it against us – they sold the Estate II so they can dominate the information system

Predatory aliens taking over the economy – hollowing out the economy –

SONG
Did you talk to me through the Sky
Did you ever wonder why
In this human form
We are always being born>?

Didi & Gogo – waiting for the frickin processers
To catch up with the process

The processors are so slow
It doesn't even GO

OUTSOURCE THIS!

Tongue Alloy – this is the way insects speak – foreign nationals – do you have a green card green man?

Aliens from Above:

HIGH LEVEL ADJUSTMENT –

They're everywhere - 0 ALIENS – with dollar signs – they're only here for the money – to take the green just as they took the chlorophyll – THEY are putting the planet into

Aliens live in middle management –

NEGATIVE HUMAN GESTALT!! LADY LUCK'S CIRCUS OF CHANCE!
DANCE OF SAUCERS IN SPACE. SOCORRO, NEW MEXICO.The scene spins in
DISSOLVE TO:
EVOLUTIONARY MONSTERS FROM THE ID

FROM THE IUD

INTERIOR. DAY. THE LIBRARY OF CONGRESS. THE ROTUNDA.OSCARThis could be the saucer. Maybe it is the saucer. Looks like the same height.TEDDYAre we inside the saucer?OSCARSwirl of surroundings; they are seated in a vancart, traveling through the catacombs of the Library Saucer, under the "stage"TEDDYThe library?OSCARIt's a big ship to run. This is all numbers, all events, all reality, all relationships.TEDDYHow big is this place?OSCARYou're the first to ask.TEDDYWho else would ask?OSCAR(loquacious, like a mocking voice over)It's a ship of knowledge -- a carpet ride to untold riches -- it's a magic trip --TEDDYYea, and I own it, huh?

OSCAR
You own whatever you own.

TEDDY
This ship...

OSCARYou COULD. And you must insure it. And renew your insurance - ANDyourself.
TEDDY(yawning)I gotta sleep.
OSCARNo yawning allowed. Have a good sday and that's an ORDER!
OSCAR leads TEDDY out of the cart onto the stage of the saucer which appears below them, again.OSCARLet me show you before you sleep.

The STAGE begins to lower like an elevator, brightly colored walls of elaborate inlaid tile (walls of information chips, mosaics of galactic knowledge) pass by as they descend.The stage flips and they are looking down into the Inner Sanctum of the Cosmic Computer and Saucer Seal. The Hub of the Galaxy dazzles, beyond that.

WHAT IS WRONG WITH THE WORLD?

OSCAR
It's all here -- everything in the universe. You could call it -- your Library of Alexandria -only with universal dimensions.

TEDDY
I don't want to sleep anynore.

OSCAR

AND YOU -- for your race -- you're the missing chip, the tile in the mosaic which must be put in place.

TEDDYSo that's why you want to get me back.OSCARGoing up?

TEDDYMaybe. Where we going?OSCARTo compute yourself into the future - with the others.The computer is here -- the master Program is in these vaults -- this is the -- ah -- database of the dead.TEDDYDatabase of the dead?OSCARYour trees, the ones you were so concerned with, they are the storage banks for the --
TEDDYWhat?

OSCARRacial memory. Cellular memory. Green cells.
Just as your genes contain all your knowledge and history, so these contain all the information of the past -- living and inanimate --
OSCAR drops to his knees.

OSCAR

TEDDY, I BEG YOU, TRUST ME!WITH YOUR TRUST WE CAN SAVE THESHOW FOR HUMANITY.

OSCAR dangles the amulet before TEDDY's face - it sparkles and dis-corporates him.OSCARCOME BACK AND COMPLETE THE SHOW.

OSCAREnd of the world, Beginning of the new. A little Final Demonstration to show the effects of how you live

They look into the VIEW CIRCLEINTERIOR! THE SAUCER STAGE. CENTRAL CONSOLE:THE WARNING - WHAT COULD HAPPENGRID: INTERIOR. MATTE: "DODGER STATIUM" IMPLANTED INTO THE 300' CENTRAL STAGE ARENA.The saucer is now an enormous baseball stadium.The overhead lights bear down on the field. Thesaucer PA system crackles, a tall alien singer stands and sings the Star Spangled Banner.SINGEROh, say can you see...DISSOLVE: LATER.The overhead console displays the score.ALIENS -- 9EARTH -- 8(or: UFO - 1/ EARTH - 0 -- binary digits)In the audience wedges, USHERS walk through the crowd, hawking hot dogs, beer, soda, peanuts, programs.USHERGet 'em here.Get your hot ones.Can't tell the playerswithout a Program.ANNOUNCERIt's the bottom of the ninth inning -- hard for the aliens to catch up -~ orwe'll tie and go into extra innings...OSCAR is on the mound, spitting, scratching. HASS is the catcher.He shoots hand signals to OSCAR.BILL EVANS comes up to bat OSCAR winds up and pitches, slow motion. He looks at the bases. FARO, FOSS and RODNEY take leads off the bases.OSCAR fires one at first, almost catching FARO off the bag.OSCAR burns one toward the plate. BILL swings and hits the ball. The bat glows. Thew ball flies out over left field, sinistra, becomes a comet... it goes into circular orbit around the field.UMP IREFoul ball.OSCAR pitches again. The ball leaves a contrail as it passes BILL's bat and socks into HASS's mit. The mit smokes. HASS stands, shaking his swollen hand.UMPIREStrike two!OSCAR pitches again. The pitch blurs through space to the bat, slow motion.BILL swings and connects.OSCAR disappears from the mound. He is replaced by a thirty-foot blue metal pylon, like a sculpture. Topping the pylon is aSaucer PA crackles.OSCAR'S VOICEThis could happen.Do you want this to happen?The ball sails out over the field, hit hard by BILL's swing. BILL begins to run.One of the earthlings crosses home plate. The score goes to 9-9. BILL runs for first, watching the pylon device.IN THE AUDIENCE-BLEACHERS, the head of Marong Stewart, out of his bowl, UNFOLDS atopo the tall, spindly body, with several boy Joints.MARONG STEWART catches the ball and blazes it back at the mound, toward the PYLON.OSCAR then vanishes in a vortex of energy, reverse-cone shapedThe BALL hits the bullseye at the top of the PYLON, like at a pitching machine, the release lever of the PYLON.CLOSE DETAIL: The bomb is released. It descends toward the mound, and explodes mid-air.BILL(Hold his hands up in the T sign)TIME OUT! TIME OUT!OSCAR (UMPIRE)TOO LATE. THE CALL IS TOO LATE!The fireball from the bomb rushes across the stage, up the aisles.The audience is vaporized. CLOSE on the figures as they come apart in reverse digitized dematerialization.Screams. Figures rush up the aisle to be burned on the spot.(Digitized vaporization as in TONI DE PELTRIE destruction of figure, only skin to skeletal)The CELL MAGNET is left towering above the remains of the saucer interior. Small fires continue burning, like torches or candles - a thousand points of light...A BURNED OUT BLACKENED

CINDER.INCREDIBLE SILENCEThe CELL MAGNET begins to move.SUPER ON SCREEN:"NULL SET"The end of the CELL MAGNET glows and as it sweeps, the colors of the audience appear as the audience is reconstructed in their seats. From blackened desolation to full-color audience/interior as the CELL MAGNET makes one major sweep, its beams glowing.Hubub of voices within the saucer as the audience re- materializes. Gasps of surprise and relief as they realize they have been returned to life.bbhkieerbThere is crying and shouts of anguish.OSCAR appears stage-center.OSCARIs that what you want? Is that what you want?VISUAL EFFECT: sucking of his composite shape back into a vanishing point at the center of the stage.IN THE BAR-LAUNDROMAT. FORECOURT TO THE COMPUBARSign crawl: Welcome to the Purple Penguin Poolbar. Where the possessed mingle with circumstance. Purple Hours are 11-8 daily.FREE Breakfast Sunday til it's gone.Reverent Hazelton preaching and taking DONATIONS.Buy your ticket to Hell early.We love you and your money. If you don't like the service, then GIT!!!GWENIt's all mucous and pus and what I read from the ozone, from the End Zone.EXT. DAY. THE COLORADO SPRINGS MICRO-RANGE.TEDDY drives toward the RADIO DISH. THE BRIGADE are starting across the mountain-valley.A beam from the RADIO DISH discorporates TEDDY.TEDDY is moved around the world at the speed of light, projected down into a ditch justoutside the PEORIA SAUCER, just outside where THE BRIGADE surround the saucer-theater with their threatening army.TEDDYGOTTA GET MARONG STEWARTINTERIOR! THE SAUCER STAGE. CENTRAL CONSOLE:THE WARNING - WHAT COULD HAPPENGRID: INTERIOR. MATTE: "DODGER STATIUM" IMPLANTED INTO THE 300' CENTRAL STAGE ARENA.The saucer is now an enormous baseball stadium.The overhead lights bear down on the field. Thesaucer PA system crackles, a tall alien singer stands and sings the Star Spangled Banner.SINGEROh, say can you see...DISSOLVE: LATER.The overhead console displays the score.ALIENS -- 9EARTH -- 8(or: UFO - 1/ EARTH - 0 -- binary digits)In the audience wedges, USHERS walk through the crowd, hawking hot dogs, beer, soda, peanuts, programs.USHERGet 'em here.Get your hot ones.Can't tell the playerswithout a Program.ANNO UN C ERIt's the bottom of the ninth inning --hard for the aliens to catch up -~ orwe'll tie and go into extra innings...OSCAR is on the mound, spitting, scratching. HASS is the catcher.He shoots hand signals to OSCAR.BILL EVANS comes up to bat OSCAR winds up and pitches, slow motion. He looks at the bases. FARO, FOSS and RODNEY take leads off the bases.OSCAR fires one at first, almost catching FARO off the bag.OSCAR burns one toward the plate. BILL swings and hits the ball. The bat glows. The ball flies out over left field, becomes a comet... it goes into circular orbit around the field.UMP IREFoul ball.OSCAR pitches again.

The ball leaves a contrail as it passes BILL's bat and socks into HASS's mit. The mit smokes. HASS stands, shaking his swollen hand.UMPIREStrike two!OSCAR pitches again. The pitch blurs through space to the bat, slow motion.BILL swings and connects.OSCAR disappears from the mound. He is replaced by a thirty-foot blue metal pylon, like a sculpture. Topping the pylon is aSaucer PA crackles.OSCAR'S VOICEThis could happen.Do you want this to happen?The ball sails out over the field, hit hard by BILL's swing. BILL begins to run.One of the earthlings crosses home plate. The score goes to 9-9. BILL runs for first, watching the pylon device.IN THE AUDIENCE-

BLEACHERS, the head of Marong Stewart, out of his bowl, UNFOLDS atopo the tall, spindly body, with several boy Joints.MARONG STEWART catches the ball and blazes it back at the mound, toward the PYLON.OSCAR then vanishes in a vortex of energy, reverse-cone shapedThe BALL hits the irtark at the top of the PYLON, like at a pitching machine, the release lever of the PYLON.CLOSE DETAIL: The bomb is released. It descends toward the mound, and explodes mid-air.BILL(Hold his hands up in the T sign)TIME OUT! TIME OUT!OSCAR (UMPIRE)TOO LATE. THE CALL IS TOO LATE!The fireball from the bomb rushes across the stage, up the aisles.The audience is vaporized. CLOSE on the figures as they come apart in reverse digitized dematerialization.Screams. Figures rush up the aisle to be burned on the spot of figure, only skin to skeletal)

The CELL MAGNET is left towering above the remains of the saucer interior.A BURNED OUT BLACKENED CINDER.INCREDIBLE SILENCEThe CELL MAGNET begins to move.SUPER ON SCREEN:"NULL SET"
The end of the CELL MAGNET glows and as it sweeps, the colors of the audience appear as the audience is reconstructed in their seats. From blackened desolation to full-color audience/interior as the CELL MAGNET makes one major sweep, its beams glowing.Hubub of voices within the saucer as the audience re- materializes. Gasps of surprise and relief as they realize they have been returned to life.There is crying and shouts of anguish.OSCAR appears stage-center.

OSCARIs that what you want? Is that what you want?VISUAL EFFECT: sucking of his composite shape back into a vanishing point at the center of the stage.INSIDEOSCAR waits for TEDDYHe puts on the effects suitINT. DAY. THE HOLIDOME.Ten alien "elders" sit playing Tarot-like cards. Virtual Yodas, with personalities, characteristics unique to each.
OSCAR"Saucer Roulette"Blackjack 21 -7-1l - cue ball with a corner shot - here it comes -1-2-3-4-WHY?
"You don't have to be the one to cry.You don't have to be the one to die...There is a reason, for your sensual season.
There is a reason for your century's treason –
It will be coming by and by...

OSCAR
If you could just figure out and act on your real priorities.
Crying of Humanity: "Hurdy Gurdy Man"Strains of "Wear Your Love Like Heaven." (Donovan)
"Cannot believe what I see, all that I have wished for will be."

SHIFT TO:

EXT. NIGHT.
BLACK EYES on TEDDY in the DOWNTOWN PEOR-LALA scene -BEE BONNET like covering for the head - shower caps - anti-RF devices worn by the ANTI-DIS-ENFRANCHISEDOSCARThings are - burn your money system - see if I care - you human evils -

OSCAR

Don't mess with the Program of the Show. Don't do the money thing - it wil disorient them before they're READY

OSCARYou don't know what you knowyou don't know where you're going yetten years' time in the future, well, tell mewho are you, who are you, who are you -ALTONThere are seven levels of hell.RODNEYWe are now serving number six, I think.ALTONOr sixty-nine - a local-time favorite.

Interior of a large flying saucer

OSCAR
HAVE FAITH TEDDY - YOU CAN DO IT

People wailing around bumping their hands over their heads, making sucking sounds

RODNEY
DOWNLOAD IT MAN - IT'S THE GOD-GIVEN UNI-FUCKING-VERSE!

FARO'S MOTHER, shuffling around, distracted, senile partly. Mumbling to herself

MOTHER
We love our boy.

GWEN
I can manifest anything. The alien is teaching me. I can blink you anything you want. I can create from nothing - with my mind!

TEDDY
Doesn't sound like any ordinary housewife to me.

GWENThe Hu-Man - the Hunab Sun - the center of the Mayan Cluster - way out there in the Pleaides Protocol. Communicating through the sun.SPINNING ROUND in the saucer the figures spin and roll into the central downspout -TEDDYGet back to the alien complex.GWENIt's not AN alien complex. The alien IS COMPLEX.ADELLEWho are you?TEDDYTeddy. Way in the middle of the air.ADELLEI am Madonna. I am Adelle. I am a STAR!TEDDYThat virtual star based on - WHAT WAS IT, the stage of that presence - Vega???GWENI am the Earth Other Mother. The alien chose me.The baby looks like - HIM.Big Other is here. He is all around -

(beat)
When somebody--your aging demonsTries to take away your beauty, give it to someone else. Tries to take your face, like the digital saucer.TEDDYLike the alien?GWENNo like YOU!GWENI want the world to end. SO there's nobody left but me and my child/TEDDYYou don't have a child we don't have a childGWENYes I do!It takes a Village of the Damned to raise that child!GWENI need to find Teddy - to tell him something.OSCARTeddy has -

found himself.GWENI need to do something.OSCARYea - the finale. You're the Savior Mother - you face off the Beast.GWENHuh?OSCARThe gimmick - the catch of The Show - is that even as it takes from you, and you give to it, the final resolution is still in terms of the dominant host planet culture - in this case, "final cosmology."

GWEN
What's that?

OSCAR
It resonates with what people already believe, what they come to expect, so to speak.

GWEN
And that's it?

OSCAR
Yes, and then we can all go home.

TEDDY
WE SHOULD BE HELPING EACH OTHER!

INT. THE SAUCER. NIGHT
Around the contrayors and corrimeter, MUMBLING people, SHUFFLING around in a room, lack of ENERGY. The BEAM passes by outside, traveling horizontally.

EXT. NIGHT. SPACE.

Shot of the transubstantiated TEDDY beaming around the planet on the GPS satellite system, then downloading directly to the site of the PEORIA SAUCER.

OSCAR
Live your fantasies. Transformation. Alchemy. Synergy. Trans-substantiation. INTERIOR. THE SAUCER.

The stage floor slowly rotates. Confetti falls from above on the audience members, whose costumes have changed to those of 18th century Vienna.

DISSOLVE

The dance winds down.

CENTRAL CONSOLE -

READOUT:

TAKE A CHANCE - IT'S THE DANCE - TAKE A CHANCE - IT'S THE DANCE - THAT'S ALL FOLKS!

The audience FILES TOWARD THE EXITS.

INT. NIGHT. THE FOYER

Sound of talking, murmur of post-Show conversation.

The EXITS open. The moving aisle deliver people up to the corrimeter.

OSCAR, on stage, watches.

INTERMISSION SONG
"Love is such a battle...It makes you feel absurd
Don't you know when you say "It's My City
I say..."Go to the sub Burb-

Look, look at the anguish despair
Don't breath in the polluted air."

DAK WILLARD Heads to the men's room. There is a line in front of OUT OF
ORDER signs. He is still tipsy.An USHER approaches DAKDAKWhat is that
pattern on the ceiling - the dome - of the saucer?USHERThe Seal of the
Saucer, a light-illuminated mandala similar to a...DAKI need to use the
restroom.USHERPlumbing's backed up.You wouldn't want to go in
there.DAKThis is super technology -- you don't get problems like this. You
must have other facilities.USHERAll closed.DAKIt can't be! I just gulped a
beer at that rip-off counter, and I need to take a leak!USHERYou'll have to
wait. Return to your seat. The Show is about to start again.DAKWhat are you
talking about! This is high technology. You don't have problems
likethat.USHER

Yes, we do. On with the Show.

 CENTRAL CONSOLE READOUT:THE GATHERING PLACE

VO MUFFLED
As the etheric level of the Planet ...

FARO
It's all about the TIMING. There is a reverse countdown, going toward the
Omega Point, when we have only a few months or years to rise about the
System and take out place in the Universe

BARRY
The Marong Stewart computers represent the enslavement of numbers and
money. The saucers offer the birthing to the next level of creation.

BILL
It's the 11:11 – the parity, the MIX.

ADELLE
Will you come to my parity?

MARTH

It's my parity and I'll cry if I want to

BARRY
No the end of time is no joke. Time is shrinking. The money system is
unsustainable. We need to replace with a larger exchange – on the universal
level

MAL
All these frequencies coming together – all the bio-energetic bodiess
compressed into the womb-space of the saucer – we are being pulled out of
ourselves – breakdown and build up to the next level of consciousness.

 LETTER CRAWL IN 3D BEHIND RETURN OF AUDIENCE TO SEATS

The 144,000
OUTTAKES played under credits

The OVERVIEW MEETING AREA

ELDER 1
What can we do to save this little dirt-rock around the minor sun?

ELDER 2Hey, we could put on a SHOW and teach them about evolution

ELDER 3How are we going to do that?ELDER 1I have some costumes in an
old trunk in the attic?ELDER 2What's an attic?ELDER 1The old control area
which was replaced by the cybertug apparatus.ELDER 4Whatever. How can
we get the place to put it on?ELDER 1Rent the all - we'll just go over and set
up - I'm SURE they'll letUs DO IT.ELDER 2OK, you write the music, I'll write
the Book, and we'll get that guy fromVega, OSCARshtar, to direct, we'll put it
on his shoulders, his narrow littleGrey shoulders.ELDER 3You are the clever
one.OSCARSo she is your property? Your woman?TEDDYDon't know if I'd go
thereSacred geosynchronous cellular memoryGWENI am the bitch-Goddess.
I am Isis I need no Osirius -Channel that energy - we could rule the world -
we could - win the Galactic Lottery!Push the button to end the world. Dead
and gone.Kundalini - Persecution complexion -
TO SLEEP PETECHANCE TO UNITE THE PERSONAL AND THE GLOBAL
So that what is happening to THEM is happening to the WORLD

COMATOSE RASPUTINASSUMA WRESTLERSTICKLER IN THE MUDINT. THE
SAUCER - DAYCLOSE, the CENTRAL CONSOLE, CENTRAL MECHANISM, and
the CELL MAGNET (retracted to its base)Lights GLOW from the central
lighting grid -- brightly, piercinglyLOUD SYNTHESIZED TRUMPET SOUND:
#$%&. Helmet interiors flash bright spectrum of colors.Multi-colored birds fly
around the saucer interior, flocking and veering, going over the audience in
great numbers and colors.

LOVE and FEAR -

THE INTERIOR OF A HEART

OSCAR
The child takes over the mother – like a parasite – getting all its nourishment
– like Marong Stewart Money-Baby wants to take over the world's analog
resources-

SHOW NUMBER

"HUMAN RACE"

But why change places when the only concern is death & destruction - sex
mixed with death in most minds is the nexus of Creation...It is the cross-
fertilization, the mixing and the blending, the arrangingOn the wings of Lust
comes out escape from Dust.
INTERIOR. THE SAUCER CONTROL AREA.Twenty-four ELDERS sit around the
central monitor. The figure of MARONG STEWART fades as flashes of light
and smoke manifest within the life-bubble.The audience takes their seats.
OSCAR on stage, smiles.OSCARI congratulate you all.A little girl, ADELLE as
a younger girl, crosses the stage and hands OSCAR a full bouquet of flowers.
He bows to her, and she returns to her seat.
APPLAUSE

.THE INTERIOR ARCHITECTURE NOW CHANGES, BY SMOOTH TRANSITION,
to:The interior of a Viennese Grand Ballroom.The PARTICIPANTS begin
dancing the minuet around in a circle under the central console, now a large
Chandelier.INTERIOR. THE SAUCER.It is Celebration Time aboard the
saucer.A SERIES OF ANGLESThe audience members cycle around the saucer.
Tubes descend from openings in the ceiling scrolls. They fill champagne
glasses which appear on the contrayor.

THOUGH the viewports THE AUDIENCE sees the Milky Way rising like a sun
in the daylight end of the nighttime day - it is the Mayan Comuppance - the
Apocalyptic Religious vision - the Ultimate Cosmology -The AUDIENCE raise
their glasses and toast the aliens grouped together on the stage, all smiling,
taking a curtain call, as happy, upbeat music plays.The music changes to a
waltz.GWENOh, how lovely!The Central Console changes to an immense
chandelier. People drink and talk. The stage area becomes transformed into
a Grand Ballroom.OSCAR and other aliens applaud the AUDIENCE.The
audience members minuet around the circle of the stage, taking more
champagne as the glasses circle on the contrayor, filled from the overhead
tubes.I am always and have always been the ONEWhat stops you now has
ALWAYS stopped you whenever you failed to do - SOMETHING

ONE SLICE OF THE FRACTAL DRAGON:

When you BECOME your money you are in trouble - it is a field of numbers - you may have a biological database, but are you just NUMBERS?

Do you forget your humanity through the money SYSTEM?

Through the HEART - the first organ out of the developing embryo is the TONGUE - and if you get down into your heart deep enough and dimensionally enough, you find that the same as jikiiiuiuiiiiiWard in the same configuration as the stars on the day that Katrina happenedWe are all

FACES of the TRANSFORMATION, THE TRANSITION and the PARADIGM SHIFT!

Hold space for the Evoution of your Species. It's the Human Race that you Must Win!

ALIEN MIDDLE MANAGEMENT - Options Monsters - keeping us from communicating - There are too many ways to communicate, but only one way to communicate with God

INT. THE SAUCER. "NIGHT"

The stage floor slowly rotates. Confetti falls from above on the audience members, whose costumes have changed to those of 18th century Vienna. They MINUET around the saucer arena-stage area.

CAMERA TILTS UP TO THE CEILINGS

CENTRAL CONSOLE READOUT:-7-

The ceiling plates of the saucer stage arena part and streams ofmulti-colored light, radiant-intense, pour forth. A loud fanfare of synthesized harmonics blast forth.There is a cube and within the cube sits a figure - OSCAR or MARONG STEWART -- or ??? Light obscures the features. Around this are positioned four omnivision forms, covered with light-sensors:the forms of eagle, lion, calf and MAN are discernable within the forms.Aztec or Mayan calendar, only more complicated and convoluted, covers the console which contains the Program of Creation and Evolution.Four horses: white, red, black and colorless. On the fourth horse sits the form of Marong Stewart, his spindly limbs and pale, translucent skin, wrinkled from the womb-life. SUDDENLY: THE MUSIC STOPS. A PAUSE. THEN:The interior darkens.Lights shut down, as "safety" lights glow around the perimeter. A buzzer sounds.Clouds gather overhead in the immense saucer-theater. Dark clouds release blood-red rain, the sensory conducting fluid.It is the beginning of the intrusion of THE BEAST, the FRACTAL DRAGONELDER (THROUGH VIEWCIRCLE)...for whom the saucer-womb has now been prepared, with humanity presiding over the birth.CLOSE on the fluid climbing the aisles, running feet.ANGLE on the aisle, blood-red fluid lapping up the aisle, scurrying ankles and legs.

People climb over each other running up the aisles to escape the amniotic fluid.CLOSE on GWEN'S contorted face, terrified.

GWENTeddy!SHIELA screams.

SHIELA
Have we sinned against the Saucer?

GWEN
My God, what have we done?

EXT. DAY - TWILIGHT. THE DITCH OUTSIDE THE SAUCER.In a trench-like ditch, TEDDY is recorporated in the ditch.

He looks up, BLINKING toward the sun. He nods his head as if getting a message from the Light.

OSCAR's VOICE
(echo)
Please come back, Teddy.
We NEED you.

PENGUINS LINED UP ACROSS THE ENTRANCE TO THE SAUCER-THEATER.

They are the USHER-ALIENS

TEDDY looks up, sees the saucer-door. It is a little iris-like WONDERLAND door like from Alice

INT. THE VAULTS OF THE DATABASE OF THE DEAD. SUB-SAUCER.EXT. THE PLAIN.Energy fount rises to the sky and (by CG representation) burrows to the center of the earth.THE SAUCER PERIMETER. The FLOODGATES open dousing the Plain with the red amniotic conduction fluid.

GARGOYLES (like Notre Dame) spit forth the destructive dense liquid.MOLECULAR PATTERNING on the ceiling and floor plates of the saucer arena: RESONANT VIBRATIONS.

OSCAR
Today is the day you get to see and be
Everything you are and everything you are not -
Effort - that is the key to gravitee -
The Ray of Manatee, moving in the ultramarine

Of your collective mind
To share. To do the timing right.

distracted lactic credits and BUY

DISSOLVE-PANOSCAR takes TEDDY from the truck, and dematerializes him, projecting him through the global satellite connections, and beams him down into the trench outside the PEORIA SAUCER in the moat-ditch circling the saucer.

EXTERIOR. NEAR THE SAUCER IN PEORIA.GARGOYL
ES (like Notre Dame) spit forth the destructive dense liquid.

The BEAM picks up TEDDY and steadies him, he points himself toward the iris-door.He moves toward the DOOR, looking up at THE BRIGADE on their POWER STEEDS - like cockroaches and Rhinoceroses.

TEDDY is connected to the STAGE FLOOR by the SENSORY UMBILICAL.MOLECULAR PATTERNING on the ceiling and floor plates of the saucer arena.

DOLPHINS swim through the suspended bodies, floating in the birthing fluid. Arcs of light, ascending - music playing. Watery, muffled.

TNT. DISSOLVES - the 144K ro rhw

WHAM!

The MICRON PATTERN of underlying visceral reality. The ZERO-POINT.

COMPLEX MATRICES OF BIO-ENERGETIC

TEDDY looks across the plain, through the BRIGADE surrounding the saucer, and sees the small, sphincter-like portal to the side of the main entranceway.Like the small door in ALICE IN WONDERLAND

TEDDY runs toward the iris-door - right into the Brigade on their Powersteeds -OSCAR is there with the molded body effects suit, like a space suit -OSCARThe ultimate Ruse - the ultimate IRONY - might be that even after all our work, the target population gets the ultimate cosmology they hauve always iagined -TEDDYYea? What's that?INT. NIGHT. SAUCER.TEDDY comes up to the sub-stage on the stage ELEVATOR.INTERIOR. NIGHT. UNDER THE MAIN STAGE OF THE SAUCER.OSCAR in the central sub-area, under the main saucer stage.DATA SUIT, ready for TEDDY,OSCARYou will rise now. Take your place in the action. YOUR show starts in five minutes.

Stage call, on your mark, get set - GO.TEDDY takes his place on the podium of the stage elevator. Elevator begins to rise.BRANCABreak a leg.INT. THE SAUCER-ARENA. NIGHT.The 10,000 bodies are FLOATING on the body-shroud tethers, a myriad of body-bag-figures floating throughout the saucer interior, ,which his flooded. Light still on from the amber safety lights colors the fluid a yellow-rose color.CENTER STAGE PLATEMaterializing as it rises out of the stage plate, the top of the tophat looks like a nuclear power plant cooling tower.AS the top continues to rise, a band is seen, then the brim, beneath that the FACE of TEDDY WRIGHT emerges.He is the MAGICIAN.Rising further to a full 100' foot virtual height, TEDDY holds a diamond tipped cane which dazzles with its brilliance. The DIAMOND is STAR-SHAPED, beaming out rays of spectral starshine.Sunscreen Crawl: OPEN SOURCETEDDYI am the HUMAN master magician! We are all humans - no aliens!Welcome to the SHOW.We are now AT THE FINALE.This is the big FIREWORKS display. The Big Bang. The Bang AND the whimper you're all waiting for.REACTION SHOTS : silent shrouds, silently absorbing all the sensory information. SPINNING of audience from TEDDY's POV.TEDDYThis is fire AND ice. hoar come the frost.BARRYLook!TEDDY takes the ears of the "rabbit" and pulls it out of the hat. Its eyes pink, its fur white.TEDDYDo your thing.AVATAR RABBITCartoon wipeout voiceTHAT'S ALL FOLKSINTERIOR THE SAUCER THEATERLights form in the shape of THE BEAST.The overhead scrollwork parts again, and LIFE SUPPORT SHROUDS descend on the long umbilical tubes, like oxygen masks in an airliner.The LIFE SUPPORT SHROUDS drop from the overhead arch of ceiling, zeroing in on the audience members, enshrouding them, preparing them for the Final Encounter.CLOSE ANGLE: BARRY is enshrouded and swept off his feet by the life support system. His shouts are muffled as the airtube penetrates his esophagus.The entire saucer shakes & trembles with thunder and lightning. The ceiling and floor plates glow menacingly - an energy matrix appears between the plates, filing the 100' height of the stage area with snapping arcs of pure energy.The saucer darkens; glowing amber safety lights come on around the exterior wall of the theater in the round. The exit doors clamp down shut against the invasion from outside.

EXTERIOR. THE BRIGADE.THE BRIGADE surround the saucer.OGONow we go to the egg, to see the delivery of -our savior.

TNT/ THE NBEAST CLOSE UP

SAX
The Beast will come from the saucers, and put us on the throne of Man. OGAGLet us go now, you and I....

SAXTo meet our destiny.
INTERIOR. THE SAUCER THEATER.TONE NOTE:The collective fears, doubts, self-loathings, recessive tragic genes of the audience consciousness manifest as visions in the stage matrix arena, as monster-forms.They are beamed away by intentional force-directive laser bran-bolts, eradicating them.

MARONG STEWART, THE BEAST, the FRACTAL DRAGON, represented as a Quaternion visual form, strains to be born in the center grid-sphere of the saucer arena.VOThe cosmic egg is about to crack and shed it love on an unsuspecting world.INTERIOR. THE SAUCER. ON STAGE:OSCAR faces the multitude. In glowing raiment, illuminated face, eyes gleaming, deepest blue -- with an "Elvis" collar ("The King of Kings") and virtual ear and head ornamentation, looking very gold and regal.OSCAR(mumbling)Deluge and Final Judgement...the numerolgu is exact, minus one.THE SAUCER PERIMETER. The FLOODGATES open dousing the Plain with the red amniotic conduction fluid.INT. NIGHT. "THE COSMIC EGG" ENCLOSURE.Light through multiple cracks.THE EGG OF CREATION GLOWS IN CENTER-ARENA.The BEAST FIGURE forms --" the QUATERNION FRACTAL DRAGON"**A real mathematical formation, a visualization of multi-dimensional form.Below this figure, through the floor plate, rises a cylindrical top, something which looks like the top, in scale, of the cooling tower of a nuclear power plant. It is deep black.The column in the center of the stage rises - dark, foreboding. It curves outward, taking on the shape of a tall tophat. The top of the column pops slowly like a lid - a furry white head emerges, ratlike, with pink eyes. Then, the ears rise and extend.It is the AVATAR RABBIT.AVATAR RABBIT (SUPER SFX VOICE - LOUD)THAT'S ALL FOLKS...The voice is slowed down, extended, saucer-shaking.SFX: Shuddering thunder, overlapping.The "tophat" continues to rise. Under it is the head and face of TEDDY WRIGHT. His teeth gleam, his eyes sparkle. His entire 100' high figure is visible now, in tuxedo, white gloves, with a diamond-tipped cane.SERIES OF ANGLES(note: "A SERIES OF ANGELS" - good book title)Show the PARTICIPANTS, suspended, upside down, sideways, rightside up, like corpses in a tank or swimming pool, floating yet attuned, like dolphins or whales to an inner chord receiving the direct sensory input from the TEDDY/SAVIOR...SFX: An uproar of LAUGHTER, cosmic LAUGHTER, boos, hisses...The COSMIC EGG appears, ready to hatch. A hand appears through a crack in its side, groping. Humanity itself, about to transform or lose to the Beast.INTERIOR. SAUCER.CENTRAL CONSOLEPARITY PREVAILS11TH HOURThe final dance of light and shape. Defined by light.A field of dark green. Saucer stage space.A throbbing, the heartbeat of the saucer...The heartbeat of the baby MARONG STEWART...A yellow orb grows, splits, extends within the field of green, thinning out over the audience area appears a light white...CONSOLE-777-A rupturing sound accompanies a rift which appears on the surfaceof the egg...A misshapen hand extends outward - an appendage of MARONG STEWART, The Beast...CONSOLE- 666 -Or is it the hand of Cosmic Love reaching out for theparticipants, awaiting merging? The arm glows. The crack widens. Within, there is mystery. The embryo-beast of Marong Stewart, grown, ready to be released, stirs. The egg is filled with light, very dark light.A trinity of powers, pyramidic, forms -- glowing and droning, in waiting. . . .quantum trinity of light, dark and matter.CENTRAL CONSOLE- 777 -The saucer interior becomes multiplied, like reflections throughopposing mirrors, to apparent infinity, all the audiences appearing in a circle of life-support shrouds, white, around the central glowing arena of Events, the stage sphere.Movement through the matrices of the stage sphere, like large illuminated catwalks arranged in a mystical order of color and progression.CENTRAL CONSOLE READOUT-- 666 --Around the perimeter of the saucer, readouts of 111, 111, 111, 000, 000, 000 appear.bring something forward out of the DREAMTEDDY WRIGHT rises into the center of the stage Mechanism, wrapped in white robes, his tongue gleaming like a sword (the CELL MAGNET) The CELL MAGNET sweeps through the sensory conduction fluid, sluicing the blood fluid, below the floating bodies of the floating audience.T

he lower stage LAKE OF FIRE.

The CELL MAGNET slices a few of the shroud cords as they are lowered by the Mechanism, and the enshrouded bodies fall into the fire...TEDDY WRIGHT rises on a horse from the stage sphere.

OVERHEAD, the ceiling plate glows with a representation of human evolution.

A complex fractal equation which spells out the genetic code.

OSCAR
Keep it simple. Stupid

EXTERIOR.MARONG STEWART, the BRIGADE, and the stragglers who have followed them backed up by the discontent

INT. THE STAGE SPHERE WITHIN THE SUPER SAUCER.

Floating figures, alien.

DISSOLVE TO

GWEN floats from her life-support tether toward the central stage area.

Vortices of energy fount from the stage to the bodies and configurations forming in the central area.

ABOVE THE STAGEGwen floats, ready to deliver. The beast-dragon (fractal dragon)-- seven heads, ten horns and seven "crowns" of light -- the dragon which gives the beast power.

SUPER ON SCREEN:
THE MERGING

INTERIOR. THE SAUCER.The energy bonds between the people become radiant-intense as the 7,992 audience participants become bonded by the laser unity - force lines from the collective bodies rise to meet at a point outside the saucer, at infinity, and burrow to the center of the earth, to the gravity center.EXT. EVENING.The energy founts from the saucer rise into the sky and burrow into the earth in a CG-generated vision of unity. The force-lines extend over the horizon.

LONG PULL BACK TO ABOVE-EARTH POINT OF VIEW (THE EARTH BECOMES A CIRCLE)In dazzling force lines, the energy founts bond the saucers together around the world.

FURTHER POINT OF VIEWThe planet, networked and crisscrossed by the laser bonding beams, in foreground, connected by energy bonding to other planets in an immense CHAIN OF PLANETSEVEN FURTHER POINT OF VIEWThe Galactic Hub, from which emanates the connecting bonds, a cluster of planets, thousands of them, united in a Universal Bonding of Free Planets..The galaxies spin through the void; the planets are connected on the energy plane by the common bonding.. .a dazzling, Eastern pattern of planets in an immense, dizzying mandala...THE TRANSFORMATIONThe saucer on the plain, surrounded by the Brigade - the lights of the Brigade's eyes are bright...ready to plunder, but they feel the energy of the higher consciousness bonding happening within the saucer, around the world, throughout the galaxy and the universe.DOUBLE DISSOLVE TOInterior, the saucer. HIGH OVERHEAD VIEW of the seats around the central stage in a grand circle - the stage is same apparent size as the earth in the previous space view of earth.SFX: a great rushing of fluid as the outside gates open in the saucer, releasing the conduction fluid out onto the planeEXTERIOR. WIDE ANGLEshows the bursting of red fluid from the saucer portals in slowmotionVARIOUS ANGLESthe fluid floods the plain, dousing the BRIGADE on their horses, knocking them down, flooding them away, etc.INTERIORThe saucer is drained - the PARTICIPANTS are back in their seats.SEVERAL DISSOLVESshow the retraction of the body shroud support systems, the superseats acting to succor the audience members back to health, taking several hours. The circular motif of the saucer again echoes, compositionally, the circular view of earth beforeTEDDY'S genes now release to the floating audience the full genetic message of transformation. The Choice.COMPUTER GRAPHIC:Detail of the unrolling, recombining, and reconstruction of the genetic code, pulled from the body of TEDDY WRIGHT and the surviving audience members.

:THE END OF TIMEFurther CRANE up to SPACE. A huge translucent ship, filled with growth and light. In a ratio of 1:40, 199 audience survivors gather on the perimeter balcony of the saucer, scanning the plain below. The destroyed BRIGADE float on the red tide of the conduction fluid across the grassy knolls of the park, swamp-like.EXTERIOR. THE PLAINThe BRIGADE is defeated. The light has gone from their eyesINTERIORThe PARTICIPANTS are now newly clad in red-and-gold robes with headpieces resembling rings which emit a healing light - halos like in the illuminated manuscripts of saints and of sketches of aliens who wore helmets emulated by kings and warriors as symbols of royalty, being "close to God."READOUT, CENTRAL CONSOLE:144,000: 1,000One hundred forty-four thousand in audience spheres are delivered from the bottom of the saucer pan as nuggets to the outer corrimeter in Transformation.

EXTERIOR. THE SAUCER BALCONY PERIMETER.The balcony rim of the saucer. TEDDY appears at the rim. Long exit ramps descend gracefully to the ground, where the BRIGADE members lie, shatteredEXTERIOR. THE PERIMETER ABOVE THE SAUCER MARKEETEDDY stands like a Noah on the Ark contemplating all he sees,RADIANT INTENSE Light emanated front the saucer. The ground of the plain steams.A light rain falls. A full rainbow appears in the sky, leading over the horizonTEDDY leads the thrivers toward the own-ramps which have deployed from the upper level of the saucer.EXT. THE PLAIN.Energy fount rises to the sky and (by CG representation) burrows to the center of the earth.ENDING #1EXT. DAY. THE "NEW WORLD" (NEW HEAVEN & EARTH)TEDDY takes a rabbit's foot from his jacket smiling - THE MAGICIANTEDDYWe must begin the world again, for all time...AREA 561 AFTER ENDOSCAR before the Elders.ELDER 1You fouled up.OSCARThey fouled their nestELDER 2They broke the code. They broke the shackles of Marong Stewart. Our control Opposite.ELDER 3What was the idea of the baseball game.ELDERNot a great device, in my opinion, but what does my opinion count?OSCARLowest common denominator - the Great Amerigoan Pastime. It's in their genetic memory.ELDER 1Locked in - a little excessive.OSCARWe had to demonstrate the full power of the consequences. They had never gotten it before. Living on the brink of annihilation.ELDER 2That's their choice - up to a point. If they mess up we have to choose for them.ELDER 3You'll be rainbow balled. No work anywhere in the universe, and a penalty.Three maln probation.OSCARI did my best. I got tripped up by the Ultimate Cosmology.ELDER 1What do you mean?OSCARI had no idea that the negative end was so deeply ingrained in their neuro-linguistic-imagistic makeup. The many called - few chosen model. They wanted to weed out the population on a ratio of 1:144. That's not a very good shooting ratio.ELDER 3 (SHUFFLING DATA SPHERES)From our records, they've been doing it for centuries.OSCARI miscalculated. We had finished the Show successfully.ELDERThen all "hell" broke loose.OSCARThe Inferno. The Book of Revelations. The Thousand Worlds, all that.ELDER 2We'll take it into consideration. You are dealing, you know, with some powerful cultural forces when you take on these little backwater planets.OSCARI will accept your judgement, but please let me ask you to be lenient in light of the target population's own death-wish.ELDER 1I think we are done here.CLOSE DETAIL SHOTCLOSES a a laptop computer "book" with a loud "clap" - And lights go dark - the chords to "Tell Her No" start: "And if she tells you to get closer - just remember she said that to me - tell her no -" etc.

OPEN SPACE
Two planet-like objects, earth and the Jerusalem ship, in spac, the ship approaching the planet - against starfield - as they come "closer" -DISSOLVE TO: the plain and the saucer.
ANGLE CRANE Up on the saucer, the field, the park and the strong rays of dawn breaking through the clouds over the New World, barren but full of potential.E
XT. SPACE.There is a huge shadow which blocks the sun, eclipses half the stars, moving closer to earth.The SHAPE gradually lights up, from within, filled with light, heading toward the northern continents, now blazing with light, descending from space.

TEDDY
Where are you?

OSCAR
On the other end of your telepaphone.

Already heading to the next galaxy. To complete another

Show.

TEDDY
Show me the money.

EXT. DAY. THE PLAINS AROUND THE SAUCER.The EARTH AUDIENCE looks up at the ship with the blinding light.It is like a enormous stadium-saucer, twelve-sided, squared off, blazing with light. 1500 miles on a side, it is the huge ship, the City of Jerusalem. The AUDIENCES OF THE EARTH are gathered up into it.TEDDY WRIGHT is seen leading the procession into the continent- ship, which glows like a thousand galactic nebulae, COVERING HALF OF NORTH AMERICA.ENDFADE TO BLACKSAUCER SEASON (Song over credits)SONG: "SAUCER SEASON"UFO's and cattleHere in the StarmanA levetated heifer, a communications satelliteSHOOTING STAR MANY TIMES MORE BRILLIANTBringing the cows home...It was big, Martha and me were sitting on the stoopI'm a hamburger, one of 18 multiple personalitiesMartha's my mother, yea...Hold things in the future, in the mind of the UniverseAnd the saucer and the egg, which came first?Three kids from LA, monetary gain was all the motiveBarley for Budweiser was better...A hundred windows light up like a markeeThe windows light up with all the faces...There is a time for Saucer Season...To every saucer there is a reason...The crystal amulet will show the WayThe crystal talisman transmutes time and spaceThe genetic change by the majesty of spaceShe's up in space in a Mothership...The Dali Llama was in the Ashtar CommandNow he's down on earth leading the band...He's down there and she's up in spaceLet's go baby to that placeGarble the babble in the galactic theaterThe universe on center stageComing around to the end of the age - yeaLOOK FOR THE NEXT SAUCER SEASON

www.ingramcontent.com/pod-product-compliance
Lightning Source LLC
Chambersburg PA
CBHW061532050726
47593CB00002B/759